RYDER

An MC Romance (Outlaw Souls Book 1)

HOPE STONE

GET FREE BOOKS!

Join Hope's newsletter to stay updated with new releases, get access to exclusive bonus content and much more!

Join Hope's newsletter here.

Tap here to see all of Hope's books.

Join Hope's Readers Group on Facebook.

PROLOGUE

Ryder

Cookies Make Everything Better

"Robert Steven Hernandez, you do not walk out on me when I am talking to you." My mother was standing in the kitchen, one hand on her hip, waving a wooden spatula at me.

"I thought we were done," I mumbled. I was not in the mood for another lecture from my parents, so I just stared at my shoes.

"Robert, listen to your mother and don't sass her." My dad sat at the kitchen table frowning at me over his reading glasses. He'd stopped reading the sports page when my mom started in about my grades.

"You know you're never going to get into a first rate university if you keep getting Bs in science. There has never been a..."

"Yeah, mom. I know. There has never been a Hernandez to go to college. The entire future of the family depends on me. Blah blah blah."

"Robert..." my dad's voice was stern and I knew I'd better knock it off.

The thing was I was just two weeks shy of my 18th birthday and I'd already sent off my college applications. It didn't matter as much if I got a B in science or not. The colleges were going to make their decisions on the grades I'd already gotten. My GPA and SAT scores should be high enough to get me into at least a few of the schools I'd applied to. But there was no way I could explain that to them. They had been obsessed about me going to college ever since I started Kindergarten.

"What about me?" My sister Lily came into the kitchen holding a bag of Sour Patch Kid candy and stuffing them into her mouth. "Why can't I be the academic future of the family. I'm smarter than Robert is." Her dark curls bounced as she plopped down on a chair next to Dad.

"Hey!" I protested, but we all knew she was right. My 11 year old sister was one of those people for whom school was easy. Where I had to study my ass off to get As, she sat there watching TV and barely studying and got perfect grades. "Just you wait until you're in high school," I would tell her. "You'll see who's smarter."

"Whatever..." my mom said, turning back to whatever she was cooking on the stove. "It doesn't matter who is smarter. Robert, you need to call that girl you're seeing and tell her you're staying in tonight. You need to study."

"That girl I was seeing" was my girlfriend of two years, Zoey Palmer. She and I met in English class our sophomore year and had been together ever since. We'd had sex the night of the Junior prom--both of us had been virgins--and everyone expected us to end up married. We'd applied to the same colleges and I didn't see any reason to change anyone's mind. Marriage was something for later on, and if my whole life was mapped out for me, I was fine with it. I was more interested in playing Grand Theft Auto and bumming rides on my best friend Charley's motorcycle. I'd been asking my parents if I could save up for one, but they kept saying it was too dangerous. "We don't want to go to your funeral," they said every time I asked. It was irritating, and as soon as I went off to college I was getting a bike.

"Fine, Mom. But if I have to cancel on Zoey then you have to make me cookies. It's only fair." I grinned at her and wagged my eyebrows at my dad, who just smiled and went back to the newspaper.

My mom turned around and smiled, smacking me on the butt with a dishtowel. "Fine. Get upstairs and study. I'll bring them up to you later."

As I climbed the stairs to my room, I could hear Lily cajoling Mom. "Can I help? I want to help make cookies. You never use enough chocolate chips."

Whatever It Takes

"Go to bed." My sister was bugging the shit out of me.

"You can't make me." She was standing in the doorway to my bedroom in the strangest pajamas I'd ever seen.

"You look like Big Bird. Go back to your nest." I was on the phone with Zoey who had gotten accepted to UC San Diego and wanted to know if I'd gotten my letter yet. It was our first choice, because it was close enough to home that we could still make the two hour drive to LA, but far enough that we could be away from our families.

"And you look like Oscar the Grouch." She tried to jump up to the pullup bar that was hanging on my door. "Besides, Mom and Dad said you're supposed to be babysitting me while they are out for their anniversary, not on the phone with your girlfriend."

Just then, a loud crack of thunder boomed and the lights

flickered off for a second. It had been raining hard all night and I knew that Lily was afraid of storms.

"Zoey, I have to go. I'll call you later, okay? I'll let you know if the letter comes tomorrow."

I hung up the phone and stood up, stretching. "Do we have any cookies left?"

Before she could answer, the doorbell rang. That was definitely strange. Who would be ringing the doorbell at this time of night?

I looked out my bedroom window and saw the flashing lights of a police car. "Lily, you stay here. I'll go get the door."

"But..." she protested.

"Lily. I mean it. Stay here."

I had a very uneasy feeling as I took the stairs down two at a time. The doorbell rang again.

Looking through the peephole, I spoke through the door, just like my Mom had taught me to do. "Yes?"

"Robert Hernandez? It's the police. Can we speak to you for a moment?"

"Can you hold your badges up so I can read them please?"

The officers did and they looked legit to me so I opened the door. There were two of them, both wearing rain slickers and I could see the squad car lights reflecting off of them. The way the lights reflected was something I would actually remember about this night for the rest of my life.

The woman officer spoke. "I'm afraid there's been an accident."

The next couple of weeks went by in a blur. Who knew that there would be so much to do? And everyone was looking at me to make decisions about things when I didn't know what the fuck to do.

"Do you know if your parents had a will?"

"Do you want to have a joint funeral or separate ones?"

"Do you have any relatives who could come and stay with you for awhile?"

I wanted to scream. I wanted to slam the door in all of their faces and tell them to leave me the fuck alone. No, we didn't have any relatives. Both of my parents were immigrants. Lily and I were first generation Americans and we'd never met our parents' families.

The look on Lily's face when I'd gone back upstairs after the police left that night... How do you tell your little sister that your parents had both been killed in a car accident on the way home from their anniversary dinner? "Oh, hey, sis. We are all alone in the world now. You and me. I am a high school kid who doesn't even know how to use the appliances in the house, but our parents aren't coming home again." How do you say that?

I'd had to find a way.

So, I'd held my sister as she cried. I made decisions that no kid should ever have to make.

The funeral was small and over quickly. Not too many people had come, largely because my parents kind of kept to themselves. There were some coworkers of my dad's who came from the plant he worked at. And my mom's friends, her hairdresser, and some of our neighbors. Mostly, everyone stood around looking awkward and sad, not wanting to look us in the eyes. It was as if they thought if they didn't see it, it couldn't happen to them.

And now, two weeks later, the well meaning neighbors had left us with their casseroles and condolences, and Lily and I sat at the kitchen table on my eighteenth birthday trying to figure out what the hell we were going to do.

I wasn't too surprised that my folks didn't have a will. We weren't exactly rich. We'd been renting our house for as long as I could remember, and when I'd gone through my dad's checkbook I realized that we only had a couple of months' money in the bank. I didn't think we were going to be able to afford to stay here, and I wasn't sure I wanted to. It was going to be hard enough to learn to live without our parents without their ghosts and memories following us around the house.

Instead of lighting birthday candles, I took a match and burned the acceptance letter I'd gotten from UC San Diego. I wasn't going to be the first Hernandez to go to college. I'd be lucky to graduate high school at this point.

"Am I going to go into foster care, Robert?" Lily sat next to me looking terrified. Her big brown eyes were red and puffy from crying. She looked so much like Mom that it was uncanny.

"No way. I'm 18. That lawyer said that I could be your guardian. I just have to get a job and prove that I can take care of you."

"What kind of job?"

"I don't know, Lily. But I'll take whatever kind of job I have to. You are NOT going into foster care." I put my hand over hers. "I promise."

Born to Ryder

"So, kid. It says here you don't have any work experience?" The man was sitting across a dingy metal desk looking at the template form application I'd filled out. His office was crammed full of the kind of things you'd expect to see in the office of an auto shop owner.

A metal file cabinet was stuffed in the corner, with auto supplies in boxes everywhere. There was a license in a cheap frame hanging crookedly on the wall that said Ortega's Autos and his name, Paul Padillo. The desk was littered with invoices, bills, about a million pens, and a couple of half-drunk cups of coffee.

His tanned face had deep set lines and his brown eyes were starting to sink back in his face from age. He had salt-and-pepper hair that was thick and unruly, and broad, calloused hands from a lifetime of manual labor. He was frowning and rubbing the back of his neck, apparently unhappy about my lack of work experience.

I'd been looking for a job for several weeks, and it was no big shock that not many high paying jobs wanted to hire an 18 year old kid whose only job experience was working one summer at Taco Bell.

That's why when a friend of mine said that an auto shop in La Playa was looking for an apprentice mechanic, I drove down here.

"I do have some work experience, sir, but it's in the food industry. But, you see, I am a hard worker, and I am..."

He looked at me and asked me, "Look, there's something I don't understand here. You look like a bright kid. You're driving a nice car." He nodded at my parents' almost-new Nissan outside the window. "You don't even live around here. Why do you want a job as a mechanic's apprentice in some dumpy auto shop in a strip mall in La Playa? Shouldn't you be going off to college or somethin'? Did you knock up your girl-friend, or what?" He must have thought that was funny because he laughed a throaty, smoker's laugh.

"Actually, Mr. Padilla..."

"Padre. Everyone around here calls me Padre."

"Actually, Padre, my parents were killed about two months ago in a car crash and I need a job so that my little sister doesn't have to go into foster care. If I get this job, I'll be looking for an apartment near here. My parents were renting a house in a nearby city, but we can't afford to stay there."

The smile fell from his face. "Oh, I'm sorry. That's a rough break, kid."

I was about to cry, and really didn't want to so I started to look around for something to distract myself. "Oh, you ride?" I nodded to a photo of Padre and a group of guys on motorcycles. They all had the same jackets on and so I guessed it was an MC.

"What? Oh yeah. We have a club. Called Outlaw Souls. The name don't mean nothin' though. We ain't outlaws and we don't got souls." He laughed again at his joke. "Do you ride?"

I shook my head. "Naw. I wanted to learn but my folks always said it was too dangerous."

"Not if you do it right, it ain't." The metal chair he was on scraped the floor as he pushed it back from the desk and stood up. "I tell ya what, kid. Let's give it a shot. You can train under my best guy, Chalupa."

"His name is Chalupa? Like the food?"

"His real name is Robbie, but we all have nicknames around here. And since you want to learn how to ride a bike, let's call you Ryder. In a couple months, if all goes well, we might even let you prospect into the club."

I wasn't too sure about having a nickname, but then again it might be a good fresh start. "Thank you, Padre. I appreciate it."

"Oh, and one other thing. We all live in the same apartment complex on the north side of town. My old lady and I own the building and this way we can keep the rent low. If you and your sister want, we have a one bedroom available."

"That would be amazing!" I couldn't believe my luck. A job and an apartment in one day. And I might even be able to join an MC in a few weeks.

As I walked out of Ortega's Autos, I felt better than I had in weeks. Even though the life I'd planned as Robert Hernandez was never gonna happen, maybe the one I'd have as Ryder Hernandez would be even better.

"So you're what? Just moving to some apartment in La Playa?" Zoey didn't sound too happy about this at all. I didn't want to tell her that it was North La Playa, the worst part of town. "What about our plans, Robert? What am I supposed to do now?"

I felt a surge of rage. "Our plans? OUR PLANS? Gee Zoey. I'm sorry that my parents being killed is putting a crimp in your plans. I tell you what. You go off and live in the dorms and live the life that we were supposed to live and I'll become a fucking auto mechanic and try and raise my little sister in a shitty fucking neighborhood. How does that sound for a plan?" My hands were shaking as I hung up the phone.

Her face flashed on my phone as she instantly called back, but I didn't want to talk. I set the phone down and went into Lily's room. She was laying in bed, facing the wall. Her favorite poster of Gerard Way, lead singer of My Chemical Romance was on the desk next to the other posters she'd already taken down.

"Hey Lil." I came in and sat down on the bed, and she attempted to hide a sniffle.

"Hey, Robert."

"Ryder. I have a new name now, remember?"

"Right."

There were a few moments of silence and then she said, "I don't want to move. I want to stay here."

I put my hand on her back. "I know. I don't want to move either. But, look at it this way. It'll kind of be like that summer camp we went to a few years ago except no counselors or grownups. Just us."

She flopped over and I could see she'd been crying. "I'm scared. What if I hate my new school? What if it's harder?"

"You of all people are going to be fine with school. Besides. You are going to be the first Hernandez to go to college."

I felt a tightening in my chest as I said that, but I didn't let it show on my face.

"Yeah. I am." She sat up and wiped her face.

"I know just what you need."

"What's that?"

"You need pie." She was obsessed with pie. Most years, she had it instead of birthday cake.

"I do need pie. Pie solves everything." She smiled weakly. "Thank you Rober...Ryder."

It was still weird hearing that name, but I kind of liked it. It sounded stronger and tougher than Robert.

"Maybe we should give you a nickname, too. We'll call you Pumpkin Pie."

"Uhhh, no. But I will take some for dessert if you're offering."

Customer Service

I was halfway under some lady's Mazda and was changing her oil when I heard her talking..

"Have you seen the new guy they hired? Seriously hot. " It sounded like she was on the phone, standing just outside the garage door. "Yeah. I might just have to start getting lubed up more often." Her laugh sounded like a cackle, and I sure the hell hoped she wasn't talking about me. "I'm not trying to be a cougar or anything, but seriously..."

I'd been working at Ortega's for a couple of months, and the job was going pretty well. Lily and I moved into the apartment and even though it was completely different from the house we'd been renting, the complex had a pool and even a small gym. I'd given Lily the one bedroom and I was camping out on the couch. She'd decorated her room pretty similar to the way she'd had it at home, and was starting to make some friends in her new school. It was an adjustment for us both, to say the least, but it was a hell of a lot better than being separated.

Turns out, most of the guys who worked here were in that MC Outlaw Souls. They all hung out after work at this place across the street called The Blue Dog Saloon. I was still underaged but it didn't matter because after I found out that the guy who killed my parents was drunk, I vowed to never touch another drop of alcohol again as long as I lived. So, mostly, I'd just go over there, sit in the back, drink coffee, and watch and learn.

Padre had really taken us under his wing and made us feel like we had an extended family. Every weekend we'd all have barbecues and watch sports in the common area of the apartment complex.

I was even learning to ride, and I loved it. There was nothing better than the feel of a powerful machine between your legs. I was saving some of my paycheck so I could buy a bike of my own. I wouldn't say I was happy, but I could say that I was making it through. That was as good as we could hope for at this point in time.

I finished changing the oil and slid out from under the car. We didn't have those big oil changing bays like the bigger shops had. Ortega's was a small operation and so we had to do everything old school. I pulled the car out to the parking lot next to the service bay and went to where the owner was standing.

Chalupa was on the phone with someone and nodded to me that it was okay to give the lady her keys.

"Here you are, ma'am." I wiped my hands on a towel before handing the keys to her.

"Thank you...Ryder," she said, as she leaned in to read my name on my shirt. "You know, I always like to tip when I receive good service."

I knew what she meant but decided to play dumb. "Oh, we don't accept tips here, ma'am. It's our job to give you outstanding service."

"Well, I can think of a few other services I need." She was really coming on strong.

"Oh that's wonderful news. I can show you our line of air filters."

"No, that's not what I meant. I was hoping that..." She was getting a little flustered now, and I could see Padre grinning at me from the office.

"Oh yes. And if you would like to make an appointment we can flush out your fuel line for only $79.95." I gave her an overly large smile that made me look like an idiot.

Irritated, she just snatched the keys out of my hand. "Thank you. I'll think about it."

As she stomped off to get into her car, I walked back to the service bay.

"That was some pretty funny stuff there, kid," said Padre. "What? You didn't want to hit that?"

The woman was too old and too... phony for me. "Naw. She's not my type."

"I don't think she was looking for a white picket fence thing, Amigo." Chalupa was putting tools away. "Besides. Didn't your girlfriend dump you?"

I must have winced when he said that because he apologized. "Sorry, man. It's her loss."

It was true. Zoey broke up with me before she left for San Diego. Honestly, it was fine. I had way too much going on, and we'd been fighting nonstop since the accident. I just wanted to focus on learning my job, taking care of Lily, and learning to ride.

"No worries, bro. I don't have time for girls anyway." I could feel Padre staring at me from the doorway of his office.

"Kid," he said, grabbing two sets of keys and tossing me one. "Let's go for a ride."

My eyebrows shot up in surprise. It was the middle of a workday and he wanted to take a ride? "Sure thing, Padre."

I wondered where we were going.

Family 2.0

"What can I get ya?" An overweight waitress with a too-tight t-shirt that said "Tiny's" on it was standing at our booth looking at Padre.

"I don't know, Julie. What should I get?" Padre smiled at her and I had the feeling this was some kind of an inside joke.

"Padre. You always get the same damn thing."

"Then why do you bother askin'" he said, sliding the menu back over to her.

"What about you, hon?" She looked at me.

"How much is the meatloaf special?" I hadn't had meatloaf since my mom made it last year.

"Don't worry about that, kid. This one's on me," Padre said, as the waitress walked away.

We'd taken our bikes a short distance down Berry Avenue to this diner across the street from The Blue Dog Saloon. It looked like it used to be an old Spires or something, and I was sure there had to be some kind of back story, since Padre knew everyone in the place.

"So, how're ya likin' the job?"

"I like it. It's really satisfying to fix car problems."

"You're good at it, too. You've got a good mind. You know how to think problems through."

"Thank you." I wasn't sure what else to say, so I just waited.

"I had a couple of things I wanted to talk with you about, outside of the shop."

"Okay?"

"First. I heard what you said about not having time for girls." He leaned in, speaking in a lowered voice. "That don't mean you shouldn't make time for women." He put the emphasis on the word "women."

"I don't think I understand."

He cleared his throat. "Look. I never had a son. Me and my old lady tried for kids but we couldn't have 'em. But if I did have a son, I'd have made sure he knew what to do when it came time to... be with a woman."

I felt my cheeks flush with embarrassment. "Oh. That. Well, I know about that stuff. Zoey and I..."

"Kid, look. I'm sure your girlfriend was nice and all, but that's not the kind of thing I'm talkin' about. I ain't talkin' what a teenybopper girl wants. I'm talkin' a grownass woman."

"Like that one today at the shop?" I was confused. Did he want me to date customers?

"Hell no." He leaned back as the waitress set down a cheeseburger and fries and a soda. She then put down a delicious smelling meatloaf and mashed potato plate in front of me. "Listen. I gotta lady friend that I used to know from before I got married. She owes me a favor. Why don't you go over there and... talk to her. She's real pretty and I think you two could be close. If you know what I mean."

"Are you telling me that she's a..."

"No, no. Nothin' like that. But she's a close friend of mine and I think she might help take your mind off everything." He slid over a piece of paper with the name Sofia and a phone number on it. "If you feel like it, give her a call and tell her Padre gave you her number."

I took the paper because I didn't want to offend him. But I really doubted I would call.

"Here's her photo." He was holding up his phone and showed me a picture of a busty Latina. She was gorgeous and I felt my jeans starting to get tight. "Just keep the number handy, okay kid?"

I put it in my wallet and then took a big bite of meatloaf. It was delicious, but not as good as my mom's was.

Out of the corner of my eye, I saw two teenage girls staring at us and giggling. I mean, I was technically still a teenager and those girls were probably not much younger than me. But I'd already grown up a lot in just the past few months since my parents had been killed. I might have been interested in girls like that before, but now they just looked immature and silly.

"Here ya go, hun." That waitress Julie set down a banana split in front of me and winked at me. "On the house."

"Hey, where's my dessert?" Padre asked.

"You look like you've had more than enough dessert, Padre. This young buck is still growing." She playfully smacked Padre. "You need to be done growin'."

As she walked away and I took my first bite of ice cream, Padre leaned in. "There is one other thing I wanted to talk to ya about."

I had my mouth full so I just nodded.

"I met up with the brothers of Outlaw Souls last night and we all voted to invite you to prospect for us."

I swallowed so fast I almost felt brain freeze kick in. "Oh wow!"

"But, there's some stuff I need to tell you first. About the club."

I'd never belonged to a club before. I mean, I was in a photography club for a few weeks in high school, but that was mostly for my college applications. I never went to meetings.

"What do you know about MCs?" he asked.

"Uhhh... you guys all get together and go on rides? Have meetings and stuff?"

"Yeah. We do that. We also put on Fun Runs and do shit for charity. But there's another side to the club too. One that's... let's just say it's less official."

I was confused. "You mean like..." I lowered my voice to a whisper, "...drugs or guns or stuff?" Zoey had watched that show Sons of Anarchy a little bit and told me about it. Wouldn't she just shit if I became like that?

"I don't want to get into specifics, but lemme just say that it's more than just riding to Vegas and having meetings. Joining the Outlaw Souls is kinda like joining the Marines. It's a lifetime commitment. It's about being loyal to your brothers no matter what shit goes down. Sometimes you gotta do shit you never thought you'd do. But you do it because you're asked to do it. We are more than a club. We are a band of brothers. We're family."

I set my spoon down and leaned back, and I looked out the window. In the dirt parking lot, I saw the two bikes--Padre's and the one I'd ridden here. Across the street I could see a couple of other guys walking in to The Blue Dog Saloon.

"You don't have to say yes to any of this. We got plenty of guys who want to prospect with us. I just wanted you to understand what it means to be one of us. If that's not your thing, no worries. Your job is secure. We keep all that shit separate. The Outlaw Souls is a separate business, and the brothers all profit share, if you know what I mean."

I thought about Lily and what this would mean for her. On the one hand, I didn't know if it was the right thing to potentially expose her to illegal shit. On the other hand, was I really going to be able to support her on a minimum wage job as an auto mechanic?

Joining the club would give us back a family. Sure, it's not the same as getting back Mom and Dad. But it would be more than just the two of us.

I could shield her from whatever I needed to. As far as she would be concerned, Outlaw Souls would be just a club. Fun Runs and Turkey Trots.

Padre was just looking at me, watching me think. "You don't have to give me an answer now, kid. You can think about it."

I pushed the banana split to the side of the table. I didn't need any more time to think. Every fiber of my body told me what my answer was.

I leaned forward, looked Padre right in the eyes and said, "I'm in."

RYDER

5 Years Later

When Lily and I first moved to La Playa after our parents were killed, all I could afford was a one-room apartment on the bad side of town. She was only eleven years old, and I was eighteen. I knew nothing about raising a kid, but what the hell was my choice? Our parents didn't leave us shit for money, I was fresh out of high school, and there were no relatives that could take her. It was either me or the foster care system.

So while all my friends went off to college, I got a job in an auto shop and tried to learn a trade while Lily tried to cope with middle school. We had no family, very little money, and were just two kids trying to stay alive.

As I sat on the beach with the sun rising behind me, getting sand in my boots, I was grateful to have the leather jacket I was wearing. It was more than just a piece of clothing that kept me warm. The patch represented the family that had taken me in when I had nowhere to turn. The day I took the job at Ortega's Autos five years ago was the day that changed the trajectory of my entire life. Joining the Outlaw

Souls MC gave me back the family I'd lost in the accident. It gave Lily and me something to live for.

My trip down memory lane was cut short by the buzzing of my cell phone. Digging deep in the pocket of my cut, I answered the call as soon as I saw it was Hawk.

"What did you find?" I asked, standing up and brushing the sand off my jeans. "Has anyone seen Lily?"

Hawk had gotten his patch a couple of years ago and made it his business to watch over the members and their families. Whenever something happened, the first person we called was Hawk, because he could find information faster than anyone else. That's why when I got home last night after the Blue Dog closed and saw that Lily was gone again, I called Hawk.

"Chalupa said that he saw her down at the Point with that Las Balas prospect again."

Dammit. What the fuck was she doing with them? She knew full well the Las Balas were bad news. Why the hell would she start hanging out with one of our sworn enemies?

"There's nothing more dangerous than a sixteen-year-old girl with a woman's body and a rebellious attitude." That's what Yoda told me the first time she ran off like this.

I growled with rage but just said, "Thanks, Hawk. I'm going to head back to the complex and wait for her there." I had half a mind to head down to the Point, but she probably wasn't there anymore. She was probably at that scumbag's place, letting him put his sweaty hands all over her.

Just the thought of that caused fury to coil in my belly. My hands twitched and became fists. That fucker better be glad I had a little bit of self-control. Otherwise, he'd be dead before he could even beg for mercy.

As I turned to walk back to my bike, I saw a blond beach bunny kissing a guy in a wetsuit and heard her say, "Let's get a smoothie before class..."

That should have been Lily. I should have been able to give her a better life so she'd be thinking about college and smoothies, not risking her life in the middle of an MC war.

"Maybe it's not too late," I said to no one. "Maybe it's time to make some changes."

PAIGE

"I don't know why you don't just listen to Mom and Dad."

My sister was sitting across from me at the outdoor table at the little coffee place down the street from our house. There was a yellow and black awning providing shade, and we were surrounded by people enjoying the sunshine and having a croissant before tennis or shopping or whatever their plans were this Saturday morning. My sister was sipping a cappuccino and keeping an eye out for cute guys.

"You're one to talk, Bailey. How many times have they told you not to drink coffee at sixteen years old?" I grinned as I said it because we'd both heard it a thousand times.

"Because it will stunt your growth..." we both said in unison, mocking our mother's voice before breaking out laughing.

Bailey was eight years younger than me, a "surprise" that my parents tried to play off as a gift to me. "You get to be a big sister!" they'd said.

It was only later that my mother admitted to me that they'd had her because my dad had an affair with one of his OR nurses, and the "punishment" was that she would finally get the second baby she'd wanted all along. Bailey and I had been as close as sisters who were eight years apart could be. Now, looking at her, wearing her MAC makeup and a tight tank top over designer jeans, I wondered if she knew how lucky she was. My parents had spoiled her because of their guilt and anger over the affair.

She took a big sip of the coffee as if to make a point. "Right, but drinking coffee is a lot less dangerous than what you're planning. I don't know why you don't just go to grad school, become a social worker, and change the world that way. Mom and Dad are right about this, Paige. You don't have to put yourself at risk to help other people."

I'd been hearing the same thing from my parents ever since I graduated from USC. *"Go to grad school, Paige. You can affect far more people with an education than you can without one."*

While I saw the logic in that, I was sick of hearing it. After graduating, I got a job at the free clinic in the nearby city of Terrance and spent my days working with women and girls who couldn't go to their parents for things like birth control or STD treatments. Many of them showed up pregnant and totally scared.

I was well aware of how lucky Bailey and I were. We were raised in Verde Hills, one of the wealthiest beach communities in LA. I went to a private college and had all my expenses covered. Bailey was on track to do the same thing, although she was more likely to go to UCLA and study law.

Terrance wasn't exactly a bad neighborhood, but it did have some seedy areas. Working with the disadvantaged community there had sparked a passion in me to help people who didn't have the country club upbringing Bailey and I had. I wanted to help make a difference where it was needed, not sit in some classroom writing papers about it.

I took a sip of my cold brew and shook my head. "I don't

know why you guys keep saying it's dangerous. It's La Playa, for fuck's sake, not Tijuana. People choose to live there!"

"Yeah, people who go to Cal State La Playa. That's not what you're doing. You want to move to the worst neighborhood in all of La Playa, and what? Get a job as a waitress? Is that why you went to college?" Bailey was talking to me, but her eyes were following a couple of young men as they got into a BMW convertible. "Hey, Chad."

They nodded hello before putting on sunglasses and pulling out of the parking space next to the café. Guys like that had no idea what it was like to work a minimum wage job for years to save up for a beat-up used car. In Verde Hills, most kids got a new car for their sixteenth birthday. Even I did, although it was a Honda and not the Porsche I'd asked for.

I sighed before pushing my chair out and standing up. There was no use talking to Bailey or anyone else about this. My family didn't understand at all. I'd seen things that they didn't want to see. I was a lot tougher and more streetwise than they gave me credit for. "You sound like Mom." I threw away the plastic cup and headed to the car as Bailey followed me.

No, if I was going to do this—move to La Playa and help the people who needed it the most—I was going to have to do it on my own.

RYDER

"Where the fuck have you been?"

I was sitting on the couch watching Cops when Lily finally came in. I'd heard the bike pull up and the engine cut a couple of minutes before, and it took all my self-restraint to sit in here and not kill the guy with my bare hands.

"None of your fuckin' business," she said, throwing her keys in the bowl next to the door. Her hair was dark brown and curly like our mom's had been, and it was tied back in a braid. She wore jeans and the same top she'd been wearing when I dropped her off at school yesterday. The material was too thin for her to have been warm all night, which meant that the asshole she was with had probably lent her his jacket.

The idea of my sister wearing a Las Balas jacket made me want to puke. "It is too my fuckin' business, Lily. You have no idea what you're dealing with. The Las Balas are bad people. When they see someone like you, they only want one thing."

She was standing with her back to me in front of the open refrigerator, drinking orange juice straight from the carton. I marched over there and grabbed it out of her hand. "Stop that shit, Lily. It's disgusting."

She looked up at me, and for a moment I saw the little girl she once was. Those big brown eyes had once been innocent and trusting. One drunk driver had ended that for her when our parents died. What looked back at me now was an angry face with a hard-set jaw and a bottom lip that stuck out defiantly.

"You don't know what you're talking about, Ryder. Scorpion loves me. And when he gets his patch and becomes a member of Las Balas, we're gonna move in together and you won't have to worry about me anymore. I won't be your problem." She stomped off to her room, leaving me holding the empty container of orange juice.

There was no way in hell my sixteen-year-old sister was moving in with a twenty-year-old prospect. I'd kill him before that happened. He didn't fucking love her, that was for sure. The only question was, why was he with her? Yeah, she was beautiful and young. Any guy with a dick would want to hit that (she's my sister, but everyone is somebody's sister and I'm not an idiot). She was also the kid sister of the Vice President of Outlaw Souls. There were tons of girls whose pants he could get into. The fact that she was *my* sister had to mean something.

But there was no point in getting into that now. Lily was home and was safe. Maybe I'd talk to Padre and see what we could do about keeping Lily from getting too close to the Las Balas. They were responsible for some of the worst crimes in La Playa. If a kid got sex trafficked or someone OD'd from dirty drugs, it was likely the Las Balas who were behind it. Don't get me wrong— the Outlaw Souls were not saints. We got our name when our founder stabbed three guys to death with a filero knife in a street fight in downtown La Playa in the 1970s. But sex trafficking and shit? That was low even for Outlaws.

Throwing the empty carton in the trash, I went into the

living room to crash on the couch. It had been a long night, and now that Lily was home, I might be able to catch a few hours of sleep before heading to the bar later for our meeting.

———

"Where the hell is everyone?"

I pushed open the door to the back room of the Blue Dog Saloon. Padre's brother owned the place, and the back room was where we held our meetings. Yoda called it "the chapel," but the rest of us just called it "the back."

The only ones in the room were Swole and Yoda. "I think they got stuck in traffic," Swole said.

"All of them?" That wasn't likely, unless there was a ride and I wasn't aware of one.

"There was a car crash on the 710," Yoda said. "Couple people killed by a drunk driver. They shut down the freeway."

My stomach tightened when I heard that. It had been years since my parents' car crash, but the memory of it was still fresh.

I yanked out a chair and twisted off the top of my Coke. Looking at my phone, I saw that it was only five minutes after. Per the rules, we had to sit here for twenty minutes and needed a minimum of five members to hold the meeting. Since I was the VP, if Padre didn't show, I'd have to run it.

"I hope they get here soon," Swole said. "Tammy is making dinner for us. It's our anniversary." Swole had pledged with us right after I did, and she was the first female member in the history of the club. There'd been a lot of arguments about whether to let women in. But she was a badass who fought like a dude, and that's why we put her in charge of security. A lot of guys tended to underestimate Swole—until she had them in a chokehold.

"How's that adoption thing going?" I asked. She and

Tammy had put in an application to adopt, but they hadn't heard back from the social worker. It was likely going to be hard for them to get approved because of her association with Outlaw Souls. Of course, there was no official association, but our MC was pretty well known in La Playa.

She'd done a good job of keeping her distance, on paper, anyway. She was the manager of a fitness studio across the street from Blue Dog. Tammy was a pilates instructor and they'd been married since it was legalized in California in 2008.

"I don't know, man. I'm gonna be old enough to be a grandma by the time we finally get this kid." She rubbed her face with her hands. "Tammy would be such a great mom. It's bullshit that it's taking so long."

"What's taking so long?" Trainer asked.

Trainer, Pin, and Moves all came in at the same time and pulled up chairs in between Yoda and me. We left the head of the table open for Padre, and I looked at my watch. We needed to wait six minutes, but we had enough for the meeting.

"For you to get me that twenty bucks you owe me from the Superbowl, that's what!" Swole grinned and punched Trainer.

Trainer looked Middle Eastern even though his last name was Lopez. He had thick curly black hair and a full beard. He got his nickname because when he was pledging he stole a bunch of ammo from another MC as part of his initiation.

I was really wondering where Padre was. If he wasn't with Trainer, Pin, and Moves, then he wasn't stuck in traffic. It wasn't like him to miss meetings. But if he didn't show in two minutes, I was going to have to start without him.

"Where's Padre?" Moves asked. He was our Enforcer and was small, fast, and deadly. The guy knew weapons the way the rest of us know the alphabet. He was the one who'd suggested we have Trainer steal the ammo because he knew exactly what we needed. Moves was also the one responsible for keeping inventory in the warehouse.

"The warehouse" was actually a Public Storage locker just up the street. We paid off the owner to look the other way, and it's where we kept the guns, ammo, and various drugs we sold and used as leverage.

I stood up. "I don't know, but it's time to start without him." I walked to the front of the room and pulled out Padre's chair. Just then, the door opened and the four patches walked in. Known as "members" in some other clubs, these guys didn't have management roles, but were active members of the club.

The recruits were likely outside acting as bouncers to let us know if there were any problems during the meeting. You didn't get to attend meetings until you were a patch.

"Okay, everyone. Almost everyone is here, except Padre. Rules are rules, so let's get started. Since we don't have a Secretary at the moment, let's get right to the numbers. Pin, how much do we have left from last year's Fun Run money?"

As Pin got out the books and put on his accountant glasses, my mind started to wander. This is what it would be like to be President. Looking around the table at the faces of my brothers and sister, I had to admit it felt good. Maybe someday I really would be the President of Outlaw Souls. I hated to think what it would take to make that happen, though. I'd looked up to Padre as a father figure since I moved to La Playa. The idea of him being gone...it was too much.

Where the hell are you, Padre?

PAIGE

My sister was looking out the window of her bedroom on the second floor of our house, watching me move out. My mother was locked in her office, blasting Ellen about as loud as the television would go, angrily pretending nothing was happening. My dad was in the kitchen drinking a sparkling water and barking commands at me.

"Don't bump the wall with that box, Paige. I'm not paying for Trevor to come and touch up paint that you scraped."

"You need to put the big things in first, Paige, and then fit the smaller things around it."

He seemed to have an awful lot of opinions for a guy who was willing to stand there and watch his daughter do everything alone.

My arms and legs were exhausted. I'd rented a U-Haul and was putting everything I owned in it all by myself. No one in this family was willing to lift a finger to help me because they didn't approve of me moving to La Playa. "You want to be on your own?" they said. "Do it on your own, then."

I was almost twenty-five years old and the only time I'd lived away from this house was when I was in college. I stayed in the dorms for the first two years and then in a sorority house the last two years. And even then, I came back home during breaks. It was well past time for me to move out.

I'd been collecting things for my eventual apartment since I was eighteen and storing it in the garage.

"Be careful of the Audi, Paige. I don't want you scratching it."

"I won't, Dad."

One by one I grabbed lamps and boxes and tables and chairs and put them in the U-Haul. I'd hired movers to load the things I couldn't carry, like my bed and dresser and stuff like that. I was going to make one trip over with all of this stuff and then meet the movers back here this afternoon for the second load.

La Playa was only about 25 miles from Verde Hills, but it was a world away. Since my parents refused to help financially, I wasn't able to afford an apartment in the nice area of town. I was staying at an apartment complex right on the border of North La Playa. I'd signed a month-to-month lease so that when I got a better job and saved up for first and last month's rent, I could move closer to the beach.

"You said you wanted an urban experience, Paige. Now you'll get one," my dad said when I told him where I'd be living. My mother just sat there, tight-lipped and judgmental.

When I finally put the last load of stuff I could carry myself into the truck, I pulled the back of the U-Haul closed, locked it, and took a deep breath. This was it. After years of wanting to move to a community where I could really make a difference to people who understood what a real crisis was, I was finally doing it. These people lived a different life than the one I'd known, and I knew from my work at the free clinic that they were often on a razor's edge between life and death.

As I pulled up the directions to my new apartment in La

Playa, my heart tightened. The neighborhood was definitely rougher than I was used to. It was about the same as where USC was located, except that I was on campus for most of my time there.

"It's not that bad," I said to myself. My parents were over-reacting, as usual. Millions of people live in neighborhoods just like this all across Los Angeles. It was no Verde Hills, but it was certainly safe enough to live in.

I didn't even get to the end of the block when my phone dinged with a text. It was my mother.

Don't think you're going to come crawling back when you're scared. You made your bed. Now lie in it.

Nice. Thanks, Mom. "No worries," I said to myself as I pulled the huge truck onto the freeway. "I wouldn't move back home if it were the last place on earth."

I told myself that it was normal that I couldn't sleep. My body was sore from all of the moving and everything looked and sounded different. Banner Manor, near the traffic circle, had looked almost upscale during the day. The front steps were flanked with two huge red doors that swung open, revealing a long, carpeted hallway. At the end of the hallway was a staircase that led to the second floor. My apartment was in between two others, to the left as you came up the stairs.

The movers had been talking in Spanish, and although I'd taken it in high school, I really didn't understand what they were saying because they were talking so fast. I did understand the word "dead" and the names of the Crips and Bloods, which were rival gangs in downtown LA. But this wasn't downtown LA and I didn't think they had gangs like that in La Playa.

But as I lay there in bed, eyes open, listening to the shouts coming from the two apartments on either side of me, the sirens going up and down the street and the police helicopter overhead, my heart was pounding in fear. What had I done? I'd burned the bridges at home with my parents and had gotten myself into a sketchy apartment in a bad neighborhood in La Playa.

Tears stung my eyes as I fought off a suffocating wave of homesickness. I wanted to be in my room next to Bailey, snuggled up next to Betty White, our Golden Retriever.

"I wonder what the pet policy is here?" I said aloud to calm myself. "Maybe I'll get a little dog or something."

I went into the kitchen and turned on the tap to pour myself a glass of water in the one cup I'd unpacked. Tomorrow would be a better day. I'd spend the day getting settled, and then on Monday I'd start my new job as a waitress at Tiny's.

Tiny's was a classic diner on a busy corner across from a biker bar, a fitness studio, and an apartment complex. I'd put in a bunch of resumes at various social justice nonprofit organizations and the waitressing job was just so I could have money to hold me over until I got something better.

"You shouldn't move to La Playa until you have a secure job, Paige," my dad had said. But my parents' disapproval of my life choices was so oppressive that I figured I'd rather be on my own any way I could. Besides, how would it look on a resume and interview to say that I was living at home with my parents in a three-million-dollar house in Verde Hills but I wanted a job helping the impoverished? I needed some street credibility.

Climbing back into my bed, I dug around in my bag for some earplugs. I was going to make this work. I knew I would.

"Well, you're as ready as you'll ever be."

I was in my tiny bathroom staring at my reflection in a cloudy mirror. The room wasn't steamy—the mirror was just so old that you could barely see anything. I imagined it was what a prison mirror looked like.

The reflection looking back at me already looked different than the girl I'd been in Verde Hills. I'd only been here two days, and to me, I looked more independent. My long blond hair was tied back in a braid. I didn't want to waste much makeup for work because I didn't know when I'd be able to afford to buy more. So I just lightly dusted my eyelids with some shadow and added some mascara so that my blue eyes didn't fade into my face. One thing about being a natural blonde is that if you don't have a tan, you can look washed out.

I didn't imagine I'd have much time for tanning. I was lucky to get the waitressing job at Tiny's, considering I had zero experience. They must have been desperate to have hired me.

"You do have a college degree and work experience, Paige," I said to the woman in the mirror. "Don't let your parents' disapproval become your thoughts."

Grinning at my inner Tony Robbins, I flipped off the bathroom light, grabbed my purse, and headed out of my apartment for my first shift.

RYDER

"Lily. Come out. You've been in there for two days." I was banging on her bedroom door, trying to get her attention over the loud music booming from the room.

I knew she was in there because her window had been nailed shut after she snuck out at fifteen. That was Moves' idea. His parents did that when his little sister started sneaking out and she's now a doctor at Cedars Sinai.

I banged on the door again. "I'll buy you pie." I knew it was wrong to bribe her, but I really needed to talk to her.

The music stopped. "What kind of pie?" she said, through the closed door.

I grinned, knowing I'd won. "Whatever kind you want. We can go to Tiny's."

The door opened a crack and I saw one brown eye and a pert little nose. "Can I get a burger and fries, too?"

"Only if you're on the bike in five minutes."

The door slammed closed as much as a door can slam when it's only open three inches and I heard her banging around in her room.

I grabbed my keys, shrugged on my jacket, got the phone out of the charger, and headed out the front door.

Tiny's was a diner located diagonally across the street from the Blue Dog Saloon. Because of its proximity to the biker bar, it was the best spot to grab a bite to absorb all that alcohol. Not that I drank alcohol. I'd never touched the stuff, honestly. After what that shit did to my life? No fucking way.

Tiny Jimenez was one of the first patches in our MC. He'd run with us for years until his wife Peggy finally got him to give it up. He bought the diner, which used to be a Spires, and now he gets the best of both worlds. He gets to hang out with bikers, but also have a happy wife.

Happy wife, happy life, isn't that what they say?

I was on the bike listening to the engine idle. This machine was such an extension of my body that I could tell just by its sounds whether or not it needed a tune up.

Lily came out, grabbed her helmet, and slid behind me. She'd grown up in this exact position—on the back of my bike, holding on to the one person she could always count on.

Tiny's was only a couple of miles away from the apartment complex we all shared. Outlaw Souls had bought the whole building and almost everybody lived on the property. The exceptions were Yoda and Chalupa. Yoda lived in a largely Asian community downtown with his 101-year-old mother, and Chalupa lived outside of La Playa in the neighbouring city of Hacienda. We'd been offering him a place to live with us for years, but he said his mother would kill him if he left home. My guess was that she didn't know anything about his association with us and he wanted to keep it that way.

Lily and I didn't try to talk over the engine, and so I gathered my thoughts about what to say to her. I had to be careful not to piss her off because then she'd shut down and not listen. But I also needed to be direct enough that she understood the danger she was putting herself in. The Las Balas were not people to fuck with.

If she really thought that kid loved her, then she was as stupid as she was beautiful. I couldn't just come out and tell her that he was using her, though. She'd probably just get up and walk out.

"Keep your friends close and your enemies closer." I could hear Yoda's advice in my mind.

As I pulled in the dirt lot next to Tiny's, I was glad to see that no one was here. There were customers, of course. But no bikes, which meant no distractions while I was talking to Lily.

We locked our helmets and Lily started talking like the teenager she was. "So in chemistry class this bitch Kayla decided that she was just going to copy off of my work like that. So I said, 'Bitch, do your own fucking work.' Like, I'm not about to get my grade lowered because she's too dumb to actually understand chemistry."

Despite her stubborn streak and rebellious nature, Lily was actually a really good student—when she wanted to be. If she was interested in a subject or felt the teacher respected her, she'd work her ass off. But if she thought the subject was stupid or had a problem with the teacher, she'd just shut down and not do any work whatsoever.

I held the door open for her and we walked back to our usual booth. I liked it because it gave me a clear view of the door and all the exits, and our backs were to a wall, not a window. In La Playa you can never be too safe, as drive-by shootings were a real thing around here. I should know. I was one of the best.

"Hey, Ryder," the waitress said as she came up to our booth. Nodding to Lily, she asked, "You want your same order? Cabellero Burger and curly fries, with a vanilla shake and apple pie a la mode for dessert?"

Lily looked at me hopefully and I nodded as Julie wrote down the order. "What about you, handsome? Anything look good to you?" She winked at me.

Lily rolled her eyes and got out her phone. It was always embarrassing when women hit on me in front of her. For both of us.

Julie Kim was harmless, though. She'd been working here since Tiny opened the place, and I honestly figured that if I did respond to her flirtation she wouldn't know what to do with it. She was all talk because it led to higher tips.

"I'll get a breakfast burrito and black coffee, please." I folded the menu and handed it to Julie. She appeared to be the only one here today, which was odd. They usually had more than one waitress on the floor. "Where's Rocky?" I asked, scanning the room.

"We hired a new girl and she's training her in the back. Why? Ya need somethin'?"

I shook my head. "No. Just curious." Rocky and I had hooked up a couple of times last year and I tended to avoid her now. She'd wanted more but, well, I just wasn't feeling it.

Julie went to put our orders in and I turned my attention to Lily. "Lil. I need to talk to you. Can you put your phone down?"

"Uh huh," she said, never taking her eyes off the phone. "Just a sec. I'm texting Jax."

"You text her day and night, Lily. This is important." I put my hand over hers. "Please?"

She sighed dramatically and put the phone aside. "Fine. What?"

"I need to talk to you about Las Balas."

Her face started to get angry again and she said, "I don't want to talk about this, Ryder. I know about Las Balas. Scorpion told me all about them and said that you were going to try and fill my head with all kinds of lies about them. I told him he was wrong, but I guess not."

"Scorpion is a prospect, Lily. Do you honestly think he knows what really goes on? He's not even a patch yet."

"And you think you do?" she said, eyes flaring.

Before I could answer, Julie came by with my coffee and Lily's milkshake.

"I do." It was such a contradiction to see her sucking on a milkshake with whipped cream and a cherry on top like a child while we were talking about one of the most vicious clubs in La Playa. "I need to tell you a story."

Lily looked at me with those big brown eyes and took a long drink from her milkshake. I'd never wanted to tell her what I was about to say, but it was something she needed to know. I'd done my best to shield her from the realities of the life we led, but it was time for her to know the truth.

"Remember when you were in the 6th grade, there was a girl at your school that was a year ahead of you? Annie McConnell?"

Lily pushed the empty milkshake aside just as Julie came over with our order. The plate was barely down when she grabbed a fistful of fries and shoved them in her mouth. "Yeah. She was killed when her family went on vacation in South America. It was some kind of boating accident or something?"

"Yeah, that's the one. Except she wasn't killed in a boating accident."

"She wasn't? That's what everybody said."

"I know. Principal Carlson met with the police chief and they came up with a cover story to tell the parents so that no one would freak out about what really happened. That kind of shit can destroy a community."

"What really happened?"

"Annie was at McDonald's after school one day with her friends."

"Yeah, we all went there after school. It's one block away."

"Right. So on her way home from McDonald's someone grabbed her from the parking lot."

"That doesn't make any sense. That parking lot is near a Target and a shoe store. Someone would have seen it."

I shook my head. "The guys who grabbed her were pros, Lily. They waited until she went around the corner of the shoe store and then grabbed her, put a bag over her head, and shoved her in the back of a van within thirty seconds. She didn't even have time to scream."

I could see the information processing in Lily's eyes as she continued eating.

"Within two hours she was on a plane to South America."

"Why South America?"

"Because, Lily. She was a pretty, white, twelve-year-old girl. Probably a virgin, too. The kidnappers sold her for a fuck ton of money."

"They *sold* her? To who?"

"That's what sex traffickers do, Lily. They sell people. They sold her to the head of a massive child prostitution ring in Colombia."

Lily stopped eating. "So, what happened to her then? Is she still there?"

"No. She was there for two days and she tried to escape. They shot her in the back and left her body in the desert."

"How do you know all this?"

"Hawk told us. He knew the guy who kidnapped her. He was bragging about it."

She shook her head. "That's horrible. But I don't understand what it has to do with me?"

"Do you know who did it? Who kidnapped a twelve-year-old girl and sold her to be trafficked and killed? Do you know who did that, Lily?"

"Who?"

"El Diablo. The very guy in the Las Balas who is sponsoring your boyfriend Scorpion."

Lily's face went pale.

"And you know what's worse? He did it as his initiation into the club. He was just a prospect when he did it."

She sat there for a minute. I could see the wheels turning in her mind as she processed what I'd just told her.

I wanted to give it a minute to sink in, so I started in on my breakfast burrito. It was a little cold by now, but still damn good. Tiny's knew how to make good food.

Lily shook her head. "Yeah, no. I don't think they do that shit anymore, Ryder. Maybe it was like that back in the day. But Scorpion says..."

"Back in the day? Lily, that was five years ago!" Before I could finish the thought, though, something caught the corner of my eye that distracted me from the conversation. Not something. Someone.

I didn't as much see her as sense her. The energy shifted in the room as Rocky and this woman came out from the kitchen. I felt her presence fill the room. It was like a fog or a fragrance that came all the way over to our table and wrapped me up in it.

My cock instantly sprang to life, straining to come out of my jeans. My eyes were locked on her like a target through a scope. I couldn't think, I couldn't breathe. All I could do was stare at her. She had blond hair tied back in a braid and was wearing faded blue jeans that hugged an ass that looked like it should be on a bike. Her T-shirt clung to a tiny waist. Then she turned around and I saw her face.

My God. Am I hallucinating? She was the most perfect

woman I'd ever seen. What the fuck was she doing here in Tiny's?

"Hello? Earth to Ryder?" Lily was talking but I couldn't tear my eyes away from the woman.

This was not good. Not good at all.

PAIGE

"So we keep the sauces right here, and when it's slow, you fill up the individual cups and put them on a tray that goes here." Rocky was pointing to a shelf stacked with trays below the counter.

My first day was going pretty well. The woman who'd hired me, Tiny's wife, wasn't here today so they were having another waitress, Rocky, show me what to do. I'd mentioned that I had never waitressed before, but I didn't think it sunk in. She was going really fast.

Rocky was one of those women who tried too hard to look tough. Her hair was dyed overly black and she had a nose piercing. Not the pretty stud on the side like some of the girls in Verde Hills have, but a septum piercing that made her nose look like a bull's. Her full lips were outlined in bright red lipstick and she tried to do that winged eyeliner thing, but she wasn't very good at it yet.

We had to wear T-shirts that said Tiny's on them, and it was a bit ironic that her giant breasts jutted out so far that you could barely read the word "Tiny."

I wasn't here to give her a makeover, though. I was here to

earn enough money to get out of the shitty apartment I'd found myself in and hold me over until I could get a real job.

But the social justice part of me felt bad for Rocky. She looked like she'd had a rough life.

"How's it going, Paige?" The other waitress that was here today, Julie, came up behind us and grabbed a couple of the sauces. "Rocky showing you everything okay?"

"Yeah, thanks, Julie. I think I'm getting it." I wasn't sure of that at all, but I didn't want her to know that. I needed this job.

"Good to know. Let me know if you need anything." She said this as she walked over to the heat lamp to grab a couple of plates that were ready.

Just then, the window began to rattle and for a second I wondered if we were having an earthquake.

Rocky pulled a tube of lipstick out of her jeans and slathered even more of the red stuff on her lips, pushed up her already pushed-up breasts and said, "Come on, Paige. The boys are here."

"The boys?" I asked.

"Yeah. Bikers. This place is a biker hangout. There's a bar across the street where the members of Outlaw Souls have their meetings and stuff. They come here to eat and then go there to get shitfaced."

I was looking out the big window that overlooked the dirt lot and saw five or six guys on motorcycles pulling in.

"Are they trouble?" I asked.

She laughed a raspy laugh that told me she either smoked or used to. "You can say that, honey. But not the kind of trouble you mean. They're harmless. Just let 'em grab your ass or brush your tits and you'll get a nice tip."

Uhhh I would most definitely not be doing that, thank you.

Before I could respond, the doors whooshed open and

several large, leather-clad men darkened the doorway. "Come on, Chalupa. Get away from the fuckin' claw machine. You have enough of those goddamn things. I'm hungry."

The guy they were calling Chalupa slid around the largest one holding a Sonic the Hedgehog toy.

Rocky wiped her hands on a towel and raced to the register to greet "the boys." I wasn't sure if I was supposed to follow her or not, so I just stood where I was.

It was like watching some reality TV show. Rocky practically sashayed over to the men, laughing and touching their arms as she walked them back to a large table. Sure enough, the Chalupa guy grabbed her ass and instead of kneeing him in the balls like I would have, Rocky just giggled.

"It's pretty disgusting, isn't it?" Julie said from behind me.

"It's...different." I didn't want to badmouth anyone on my first day.

"Can you take this pie to table 12? Put a scoop of ice cream on it first. I have to take my fifteen." She handed me a warm plate of apple pie.

"Which table is that?" I asked, looking around.

"The one with the guy who is staring at you like you're his next meal." She nodded to the side and, I'm not kidding, time literally stopped.

It was like one of those movies where everything slows down. I could hear Rocky laughing and the clinking of glasses. There was the sizzle of the grill and the smell of the pie in my hand. But the entire universe narrowed down to table 12 and the guy who was staring right at me from across the room.

It was the craziest thing, but I felt like I knew him. Not in the "don't I know you from somewhere" kind of way. But like "knew him" on a soul level. My mom was super into past lives and shit and I'd always laughed at her for it. Looking at this guy, though, I had to wonder. Why did he seem so familiar?

"Paige? The ice cream is over there." Julie pointed to the freezer. "You good?"

"What? Oh yeah." I came back to reality and time moved back to its normal pace again. "Go ahead. Take your break."

"Okay. Be back in fifteen."

I was aware of him watching me as I scooped out the ice cream and placed it on the pie. I grabbed the can of whipped cream and headed over to table 12.

The hairs on my skin stood up as his gaze went up and down my body as I walked toward them. It was the strangest feeling—as if I were being drawn into a black hole by some magnetic force.

I got to the table and managed to set the plate of pie down. He was still looking at me with those black eyes, and the girl he was with was looking back and forth between us with a disgusted look on her face. "Ew. Ryder. Stop looking at her like that."

Ryder cleared his throat and looked away. "The pie's for her," he said, motioning to the girl.

"You want whipped cream?" I asked, surprised that my voice sounded normal.

"Yeah. Lots."

I was looking at Ryder while spraying the whipped cream on the pie. I guess I must have been distracted by those long eyelashes or those full lips that looked like he'd been eating cherries. Or maybe it was the tiny scar under his left eye. Whatever it was, I was obviously not paying attention because the girl said, "Uhhh...that's good?"

I looked at her plate and burst out laughing. I'd put so much whipped cream on that you couldn't even see the pie anymore. It was literally just a mound of whipped cream.

"Oh my gosh, I'm sorry." I said, embarrassed. "It's my first day. Do you want me to get you another one?"

Ryder spoke and his deep voice took me by surprise. I wondered if he was a singer, because that baritone sound would be incredible in a church choir. He didn't look like the kind of guy who went to church, though.

"There's no such thing as too much cream." As soon as he said that, my pussy felt like it had been zapped by an electrical shock.

"Okay, y'all are gross." The girl slid out of the booth. "I'm gonna go to the bathroom while you old people finish this flirting thing you're doing and then I'm gonna come back here and eat my pie."

As she walked away, Rocky came up behind me. "Is everything okay here?" She spied the plate of whipped cream and leaned over to grab it. Ryder's eyes never left me.

"We're fine, Rocky. Leave the pie. She is coming right back." He practically barked the command at her, and she just sort of slunk away.

"Come on, Paige," Rocky said over her shoulder. "Let me show you the freezer in the back."

The heat coming off my body was so intense that a little time in the freezer was a really good idea.

"Nice to meet you, Paige," Ryder said. "It's good to have a fresh face around here."

"It's fucking cold in here," Rocky said before laughing. "But then, that's why they call it a freezer, right?" She walked out of the huge room that was filled with ice cream, frozen meats, and other things that needed to stay frozen.

I must have still seemed dazed after that strange encounter with Ryder because Rocky said, "I think it's time for your fifteen. Let's ask Julie if we can take them together, since it's a little slow right now."

I didn't really want to talk to her during my break. I needed some time to process what had just happened to me. I was no virgin. I'd dated some guys in college. I'd even gone skiing with Caldwell Blacktone's family.

But this was different. This was something I'd never felt before in my life. It made everything else pale in comparison.

What the hell just happened to me?

Five minutes later we were sitting in Rocky's truck and she was smoking and talking like I was some kind of friend, not a coworker she just met three hours ago.

Evidently she'd been kicked out of high school and sent to a continuation school that she also was asked to leave. She did a short stint in juvie for shoplifting, but the record had been sealed, which was why she was able to get this job.

"Trouble has a bad habit of finding me wherever I go," she said, offering me a drag of her cigarette.

Shaking my head no, I asked, "Why is that?" I wasn't trying to be a therapist, but my guess was that trouble didn't find her; she found it.

"I don't know. You know that guy earlier? The one with the whipped cream kid? He's trouble with a capital T. We had a thing last year, but I knew he was a problem so I got out of it as soon as I could." She flicked the cigarette butt out the window and twisted open the top to the Dr. Pepper she'd brought with her.

Rocky had slept with Ryder? That was interesting. "What kind of problem?" I asked. I couldn't get my brain around *him* with *her*.

"He's the kind of guy who seems like a decent guy on the

outside...took his kid sister in when their parents were killed by a drunk driver. Helps old people and animals. Shit like that. But underneath it, he's a cold-blooded killer. Other guys get drunk and sloppy. Not Ryder. Everything he does is calculated and for his own benefit. I figured that out real quick and now I stay away from him."

My eyes gazed out the window and I could see the biker bar across the street. Chalupa and the guys were pulling in and I could see them laughing and patting each other on the back as they walked inside.

Maybe I ought to go and check out this biker bar myself... you know...for research.

RYDER

I was sitting in my usual seat in the back corner of the Blue Dog. It was a normal day, with the regulars sitting at the bar, the day bartender Connie serving drinks, and some talk show on the TV overhead. The pool tables were empty, but by the end of the night, there would probably be a lively game going on. Chalupa and Dog had an ongoing battle and they kept winning back the same twenty bucks from each other every week. Just a regular day at the bar.

Why, then, was my mind still across the street at Tiny's? Thinking about that waitress with the long blond hair, wanting to grab that ponytail and crush those lips with my mouth...

What the hell was wrong with me?

I'd been in love exactly once. It was before my folks had been killed and it was my senior year in high school. It was one of those storybook first love kind of romances. We met in English class, wrote each other poetry, went to the carnival and made out on top of the Ferris Wheel. She was my first sexual experience and I was hers. It was supposed to last forever.

I had a girlfriend, I was getting ready to go off to college and start my own life. When the accident happened, though, everything changed. I got really angry. Not just angry—I was filled with so much fucking rage that I took it out on everyone around me.

My rage got the best of me and I lost the job, lost the girlfriend, and almost ended up on the streets with a little sister to support.

That's when I met Padre. He ran the auto shop and gave me a job, a place to live, and eventually the chance to prospect for Outlaw Souls. He taught me how to fight, how to shoot, and how to kill. If it weren't for him, I don't know what would have happened to me.

But love? Love wasn't in the cards for me again. My life was no life for a woman. I'd seen what happened to guys— and Swole—who tried to balance being in a relationship with being in the club. It didn't work out for long. You ended up having to choose one or the other. Tiny chose his wife and that's how he ended up opening the diner. My loyalty was to Outlaw Souls and Padre, not some woman.

Don't get me wrong. I wasn't exactly a monk. When the urge struck, I could easily find women to be with. There were plenty of women who were happy, like that waitress Rocky, though they always wanted more than I could give them. So we'd fuck around for a few weeks and then I'd break it off. No sense getting anybody hurt. I didn't feel anything for them, and as soon as they started to have feelings for me it was time to end it.

This thing with Paige, though. That was different. Scary different. My body wasn't cooperating with me, and that could be very dangerous for everyone. It was best for everyone that I just steer clear of her.

A ray of yellow light came in the room as the front door opened.

"Padre," Connie said as his lumbering shadow came into the room. "Long time no see. You want the usual?"

Padre's usual was a Tecate with lime and a tequila chaser. "Yeah."

I could hear the bar stools scrape the floor as he pulled it out far enough to sit on. He was a large man, but under the layer of fat was as much muscle as a gorilla. He was strong as fuck and one hit from him was enough to render a man unconscious. Even though the man was well into his sixties, everyone knew not to mess with Padre.

I wanted to know where he was when he missed the meeting, but didn't want to ask. I figured he'd tell me if he wanted me to know. But it was time for a refill of my coffee, so I grabbed my cup and went up to the bar, opposite where Padre was. The Enforcer was next to me, stuffing peanuts in his mouth.

I held the cup up and said, "When you get a minute, Connie?" She nodded at me as she slid the beer and shot over to Padre.

As she poured the coffee in my cup, I watched as Padre took his shot and then a long sip of beer. An audible "ahhh" came next.

"Hey Padre," I said.

"Ryder."

"Did you get Trainer's email about the Vegas run? Looks like we're up to twenty guys."

"Yep. Saw that." He didn't look in my direction as he answered me.

I really didn't have anything else to say to spark a conversation without it seeming weird, so I grabbed my coffee and headed back to my table. Padre was in a weird mood and if I didn't know any better, I'd think he was pissed at me for something. I couldn't imagine what it would be, though, so I dropped it.

As I sat back down, the Enforcer turned to Padre and said, "You were missed at church." The combination of the peanuts in his mouth and the heavy accent made it almost impossible to understand what he was saying.

Vlad "The Enforcer" Kushniruk came to us when he got asylum in the US from the Ukraine. It was some kind of political deal. He came here in exchange for doing some shady shit for the government. His reward was that he wasn't tortured and killed by his own government. He moved to La Playa, got a job selling cars at the dealership down the street, and graced us with his sharpshooter skills. He was the only guy in the club who was a better shooter than me, and for that reason I made sure to stay on his good side. You can only expect so much loyalty from a guy who was willing to betray his whole country.

"You were sick or something?" The Enforcer wasn't one to pick up on subtlety. Asking Padre why he missed the meeting was not something to do. But Padre would let it slide.

"Nope."

Just then the door opened again, and even though I couldn't see who it was because of the darkness of the bar, I knew it instinctively. It was Paige. I could see the silhouette of her curves against the yellow light streaming in.

The door swung shut behind her and she stood still while her eyes adjusted to the darkness. I instinctively shrank down a little in my seat so she wouldn't see me. At the same time, my cock decided it was time to come out and play. Further reason to leave the chick alone.

Paige looked around and then pulled out the stool next to Padre.

"What can I get ya?" Connie asked as she slid a coaster across the bar.

"Uhhh...I don't know. What chardonnay do you have?"

"The white kind." Connie chuckled at her own joke.

"No, I mean the vineyard. What brand is it?"

"Honey, I don't know. Not too many people order wine in here. We have white and red. We might have some pink in the back. That's it."

"Okay. I'll have..."

"She'll have what I'm having." Padre's gruff voice interrupted her. He turned to Paige and said, "Trust me. That wine is older than you, and not in a good way. If you don't want the shot of tequila, I'll be happy to take it for you."

"Oh! Okay then." Paige looked at Connie and said, "I guess I'll have what he's having."

Connie shook her head and turned around to get another beer and shot of tequila.

Paige started to fish around in her purse, probably for money, when Padre said, "I got it."

"Thank you, but you don't have to, really..." She smiled at him and I felt it like a kick in the gut.

I didn't like the way Padre was looking at her, but there wasn't much I could do about it. "No problem," he said as he looked at the TV.

"I'm Paige," she said as she stuck her hand out to meet his. "I just started working at Tiny's."

Stay away from him, Paige. My inner alarm was screaming out, but it was probably just a strange case of jealousy. He was old enough to be her father, and he didn't fuck around on his wife Nancy. Not anymore, anyway.

Padre shook her hand briefly and said, "Tiny's a good guy. We've known each other since he really was Tiny." He laughed at his own joke and then coughed a little. "I'm Padre."

"Well, Padre. Thanks for the drinks." She took a dainty sip of the beer, and then threw back the shot like a pro. She didn't even wince as she sucked on the lime.

Well, well. Paige might not be as innocent as she looks.

"My pleasure."

The shot took effect, and Paige slid off the barstool, grabbed her beer, and started to look around the room. It was just a matter of time before she was going to see me sitting in the corner, so I tried to make myself as invisible as possible. That woman was trouble, and I needed to stay far away. I needed to get out of here.

As soon as she turned to look at the digital jukebox, I grabbed my bag and headed for the back door. Connie would close out my tab for me. Just as I pushed open the door, I heard Paige say, "Ohhh pool! I love shooting pool."

Imagining her bent over a pool table with those long fingers wrapped around a cue? Yeah, definitely time for me to leave.

PAIGE

I was disappointed, I'll admit it. When I went into the Blue Dog Saloon, I had been hoping to run into Ryder. Instead, I saw an old guy wearing an Outlaw Souls jacket, and down at the other end of the bar was another guy who looked foreign —maybe Russian—wearing the same jacket.

It was really dark in there, but as far as I could tell, they were the only two there. That bartender had kind of an attitude, but whatever. I knew that I didn't look like I'd fit in, but I'd win them over in time.

After the beer and the shot, and working a full day, I was tired. I didn't really want to go back to my apartment, but I really didn't have a choice. I had the afternoon shift tomorrow at work and I didn't know anyone in town other than Rocky, and I really didn't want to get to know her as anything more than coworkers.

I stopped at the Mexican market that was just down the street from the bar. It was called Southgate Martinez and had a whole burrito bar inside the store. I made myself a huge one and got a bottle of water and a cup of mangoes and yogurt for breakfast. When in La Playa, right?

As I was carrying my stuff inside, my phone rang. I didn't recognize the number, and even though I don't usually answer calls, I was hoping it was one of the jobs I applied for. I pulled the phone out of my back pocket.

"Hello?"

"Is this Paige Anton?"

"This is she."

"Hi, this is Elizabeth Maroni from Californians for Social Justice."

"Oh yes! Hi. Thanks for calling." This was the job I'd been most interested in.

"We received your application and would love for you to come in for an interview."

"Great! Oh, that's great news. Yes. When?"

"We are interviewing several candidates and have an opening tomorrow afternoon. I'm sorry for the short notice, but our regional manager is only here for a short time."

"No, no. That will work." I had my shift at Tiny's, but hopefully I could do it on my lunch break. "What time?"

"How about 1:30?"

"You got it. I'll be there." This was such great news! "Thank you!"

I was so happy the rest of the night that I didn't even mind the sirens and the helicopters or the shouting neighbors. I had a job interview tomorrow!

I should have known something was up when I couldn't find parking in Tiny's lot. There were so many cars that they overflowed onto the street. Even the lot across the street in front of the Blue Dog was packed. I had to park at the gas station on the other corner and hope my car didn't get towed. I'd move it to the regular lot when I got back from my interview.

Walking in the door to Tiny's, the place was even more jammed than the parking lot. The waiting area was full, and there were parents and kids lined up to use the claw machine. Rocky and Julie were racing around with plates and cups of coffee, and customers were calling to them as they hustled by. "Excuse me, Miss? Can I change my order?"

"What on earth is going on?" I asked Bobby, the cook.

"Fundraiser day for the local elementary school. Every year Tiny donates a percentage of the day's meals to Carter Elementary."

"Are you going to just stand there or are you here to work?" Tiny's wife Martha was plating orders and throwing them under the heat lamp. I hadn't seen her since I'd been hired.

"No, no, of course." I washed my hands and grabbed a ticket to see which orders went to which tables. "By the way, can I take my lunch at 1:00 today? I have...an appointment."

"No lunches, no breaks today. We need all hands on deck." Martha didn't even look up at me as she was throwing orange slices on plates.

"Right, but we are legally supposed to take breaks every shift."

She looked at me, and her watery blue eyes were as serious as could be. "You gonna call the labor board? You're free to leave if you got a problem, otherwise get these sandwiches to table 24."

Tears sprang to my eyes as I grabbed the plates. I needed the interview to get a better job, but I needed this job to pay my immediate bills. I just hoped I'd be able to step away and at least call to let them know I couldn't make it. And hope that they would reschedule me.

My feet were killing me. Actually, everything was killing me. My feet, my legs, my shoulders. Even my fingers.

I'd made decent money in tips, but I hadn't had one second to sit down or even go to the bathroom. It wasn't until we finally closed at 10 pm that I got the chance to check my phone. There were several text messages from Elizabeth Maroni wondering where I was. It was too late to call now, but I'd return her call first thing in the morning.

The night was chilly as I walked to the crosswalk to get my car from the gas station. I could hear music and laughing coming from the Blue Dog, but otherwise, the night was quiet.

Maybe I'd get a package of cookies or something from the gas station for dinner. I hadn't gotten to eat and there wasn't anything at home, but I was too tired to go to the market.

Crossing the street, the awareness dawned on me and my stomach clenched in panic. Where was my car?

Frantic, I looked around. The gas station parking lot wasn't exactly large, and it was very clear that my Honda was not there.

Bursting in the overly bright gas station, the clerk behind the counter was counting out lottery tickets for a woman holding a huge soda.

"Excuse me. Do you know where my car went?"

"Wait your turn, lady," Lottery Woman said to me.

"I just want to know where my car is. Was it stolen or towed?" My heart was pounding so hard I could hear it in my ears.

The clerk didn't even look up. "I dunno," he said.

"Did you see a tow truck or anything?" Why was no one cooperating?

"Nope, I just got here."

"Dammit." I pushed the doors open and walked out into

the brightly lit gas pump area. What the hell was I going to do now?

I stood out there for a full minute looking around. My apartment was only a couple of miles away. Should I walk home? Was it even safe in this neighborhood? Maybe I should call an Uber or something. Then again, I didn't want to waste my precious dollars on a ride.

The first thing I needed to do was call the cops and see if the car was stolen. I pulled my phone out of my back pocket and walked over to the space where I'd parked the car.

I was about to call the La Playa non-emergency police number when a voice spoke behind me. "It was probably towed. They're pretty crazy about it in this town."

I knew the voice before I even turned around.

"Ryder!" I swung around to face him.

"Paige." He was looking down at me and I couldn't help but notice those damn eyelashes again.

"I didn't hear your bike."

"I'm in my car." He nodded to a VW Bug that was hooked up to a pump.

"You drive a Bug?" That just didn't compute.

"It's going to be my sister's in a month or so when she gets her license. I could only afford one car and I let her pick it out."

I was listening but I was also very aware of how close he was standing to me. He smelled like leather, coffee, and...pie? It was almost enough to make me forget about my car.

"Do you have the number?"

For a second I was confused. Was he giving me his number? Did I miss something?

"What?"

"The number to the tow company." He gestured to the sign that was on a pole right near where I'd left my car. "Aloha Towing Company."

"Oh. Right." I punched in the number and spoke to the guy. They had my car, but the impound yard was closed for the night. I was going to have to wait until the morning to get the car.

Ryder had gone back over to his car to finish getting gas, so I walked over to where he was.

"Thanks," I said. "You were right. They have my car."

He stood there staring at me for what felt like a full minute. Then he asked, "How are you getting home?"

"I'll take an Uber or something."

"Where do you live?"

"Banner Manor."

His face registered surprise. "You live there? How did you end up there?".

"It's kind of a long story. Why?"

"I'll give you a ride home." He nodded to the car. "Get in."

"No, really. I'm fine." I didn't appreciate the way he was ordering me around.

"Seriously. Paige. I insist. That is no neighborhood for you to be alone in at night."

"Ryder, look. I appreciate your concern. But it's really..."

"Get in the damn car, Paige." It came out more like a growl than a sentence.

I did as he said. It was only a couple of miles and I'd rather save the Uber money. "Okay. Thanks."

I slid in the front seat and noticed the evidence of a teenage girl everywhere. There were magazines and empty Starbucks cups, hair ties and empty candy bar wrappers. Ryder didn't look like he ate too many candy bars. He was all muscle.

"So your sister is sixteen?" I asked, making conversation.

His jaw was clenched pretty tightly, but he said, "Sixteen going on twenty-one."

"My sister is sixteen, too. I definitely get that." I kept stealing looks at Ryder as we drove. His profile was strong and the angles of his face were incredibly masculine. His broad hands had long fingers, and there was a jade ring on his right ring finger. He tapped the steering wheel impatiently, as if he were in a hurry to drop me off.

It took less than five minutes for us to pull up in front of my apartment complex. I started to open the door when he grabbed my arm. He leaned in really close and I could smell him. The scent went through my skin and my heart started pounding. He was silent for a moment and for a second I thought he was going to kiss me. But he released my arm instead.

His voice was raspy as he spoke. "What are you doing, Paige?" The words came out like an accusation.

"I'm going into my apartment." I wasn't sure what he meant.

"No. I mean here. In La Playa. What are you doing here?"

"I'm just...living here."

"You shouldn't be here. You're too...good for this place." He nodded toward the big red doors. "This is not a safe place for a woman like you. I saw you yesterday at the bar. Talking to Padre. You're playing with fire, Paige. Go back to where you came from."

I couldn't believe he was saying these things to me! "Look, Ryder. I know I look soft but I'm not. I went to school in one of the roughest parts of LA. I worked at a free clinic in Terrance. I'm not some innocent thing that needs to be protected, okay? I came to La Playa so I could make a difference, and I'm not leaving until I do." I yanked free from his grasp and opened the car door. "Thanks for the ride and the advice, but I can take care of myself."

"Fine. Suit yourself." Ryder put the car in gear. "Just don't say you weren't warned." As soon as the door shut, he sped off into the night.

RYDER

Even though I drove away, I pulled over to make sure Paige got inside okay. Banner Manor was not the kind of place a woman like her should be living alone. It was filled with druggies and criminals. And not the kind that were a member of an MC, either. At least we had loyalty and some moral values —even if most folks didn't agree with them. We lived by a code of honor.

But the kind of people that lived at Banner Manor? Those were the ones who didn't have any code and they had no problem doing whatever they needed to do to benefit themselves.

As soon as I saw the light in her apartment turn on and I could see her shadow moving across the window, I pulled out from the curb and made my way home.

I passed by the Blue Dog and thought about stopping in. But I had groceries in the car and I didn't want to have coffee. I was mad at myself for getting so close to kissing Paige earlier. For the first time in a long time, I wished I had the mind-numbing effect that alcohol would provide. Except

I didn't drink, and alcohol would probably only make it worse. That woman was getting under my skin.

I'd love to get under her skin, too...

Passing by the shop, I noticed a light on. Padre was probably working late, doing the books or something. There were only two bikes in the lot—his and one I didn't recognize. He'd been acting kind of weird lately, and if I didn't know the guy so well I'd think he could be fucking around on his wife or something.

What he did in the bedroom was none of my business, though, and so I turned the corner to head home. Lily's Chunky Monkey ice cream was probably melted already and I needed to get it in the freezer before it was completely ruined.

Lily wasn't home when I got there, so I turned on Cops while I put away the groceries. I sure the hell hoped she wasn't with Scorpion again, but I bet she was. I couldn't stand the guy or anything he represented. But it was partly my fault that she was attracted to a guy prospecting with an MC. After all, I'd been the one who brought this world into her life.

Nonetheless, she was in danger and I was torn as to how to handle it. On the one hand, I wasn't our dad, and I couldn't exactly lay down the law like he would have. He'd have locked her in her room or something. I honestly didn't know, but it would have been some parental way of handling it that wasn't my style.

I was her brother, and even though I was the one in charge and had basically raised her, we didn't have that kind of relationship.

On the other hand, the Las Balas were scary. I wasn't scared of them, of course. But Lily should be scared, and she wasn't. That was what scared me. If I pushed her away by being too controlling, it would only draw her in closer to the Las Balas.

The story about Annie being kidnapped and killed had zero effect. Lily was still playing with fire, and it was just a matter of time before we all got burned. I had to find another way to get through to her—I just didn't know what it was yet.

Cracking the top off of a non-alcoholic beer, I went to sit down and watch the show. Part of me wished I could just command her to stop seeing Scorpion. But if there's one thing true about a teenage girl, it's that they don't like being told what to do.

Maybe it was time to take matters into my own hands.

"Here. Put it in your hand. Like this." She was facing away from me, and the cascade of blond hair fell to the middle of her back like one of those smooth water fountains. She was standing so close to me that her ass was pressing up against my thighs, and I was sure she could feel my raging hard-on. She had to know the effect she had on me.

I took her hair in my hands as she suggested and looped the silky strands around my palm. Gently but firmly, I pulled her head back so it was pressing into my chest. Her entire body was pressed against me as I leaned down to smell her.

"You're not going to be able to make a ponytail if you have me pulled so close." She was smiling and looking up at me, still facing forward.

I wasn't thinking about putting her hair in a ponytail. All I could think about was getting my cock inside of her. I knew it would be as soft and smooth as her hair.

I growled in response, and I swear to God the woman pressed her ass into me even more. Dropping her hair, I snaked both hands around her front and grabbed her breasts. Her nipples were thick and pressed through the thin material of the T-shirt she was wearing. She obviously wasn't wearing a bra, and so I slid both hands under her shirt and made my way up to those perfect breasts.

She leaned her head back into my chest and moaned in pleasure. Her legs spread open a bit and I took the cue. I slid my right hand down her belly and inside the waistband of her jeans. If she was wearing panties, the fabric was so thin I couldn't feel it.

My cock was straining to get out of its confinement as my fingers explored her soft wetness. My index finger found its way to her sensitive clit and I began playing her body like an instrument. She was moaning and pressing into me, and it was just a matter of time before she asked me to do what I'd been waiting all night to do.

"Can you open this for me? The lid is frozen shut."

My eyes flew open and I realized that I wasn't with Paige. I was on my couch, thankfully covered with a blanket as Lily stood over me holding the ice cream container. The eleven o'clock news was on and I must have fallen asleep.

"Ryder?"

As I took the ice cream from her, I was dazed and a little annoyed. If I couldn't have Paige in real life, at least let me have her in my dreams...

PAIGE

It had been about a week since my car had been towed and I was lying in bed trying to sleep, but my irritation and anger were growing by the minute.

I know people like to have friends over on the weekends. I get that you want to have a party now and then. But this was ridiculous. My neighbors treated this apartment complex like it was some kind of nightclub on the weekends. Ubers and Lyfts pulling in and out at all hours of the night. People walking up and down the hall outside my apartment, laughing and talking in full voice—not even attempting to be quiet. Many nights this went on until 3am, and it had been happening every Friday, Saturday, and Sunday night since I moved in.

I'd tried calling the property management company and they never even called back. I called the cops who said they would "send someone out." No one came. I would go and talk to them myself, but after what everyone had said about this neighborhood, frankly I was a little afraid to confront them.

So instead, I lay here at 1:00 in the morning listening to some chick puke on the sidewalk below and her friend telling her that she needed food and they should go to Tiny's. I didn't have the energy to tell them that Tiny's was closed. I'd closed it myself when I left work earlier.

Angrily rolling over, I grabbed my phone to check Facebook or something until I could sleep. Before I got the chance, though, it rang. As soon as I saw the name and face on my caller ID, my heart froze. It was Bailey. Why the hell was she calling me at 1:00 am?

"Bail? Is everything okay?" My heart was pounding in my ears. What if it were something with Mom or Dad?

"Paiggggee." I heard a lot of laughing and loud music. "Can you hear me?"

Unless Mom or Dad were having a medical emergency at a nightclub, this wasn't about them. "I can hear you. What's going on?"

"Paige?" The music was booming so loud we could barely hear each other.

"Bailey. Yes. I'm here. Can you hear me?" I felt like that guy on the Verizon commercial.

"The quesssion is can YOU hear ME. I'm the one who called YOU? 'Member?"

Good lord. She was drunk off her ass. "Bailey, where are you?"

"I'm here. But the thing is, I need to go home, but I can't go home because, I don't know if you can tell this or not, but I had a couple of beers or two tonight and Mom would kill me if she knew. She'd say I was turning out just like you." She then hiccuped and said, "No offense."

"Bailey. Where is 'here'? Where are you?" I figured I should at least get a location in case the call got interrupted or something.

"Paige?" She was slurring her words. "Can you hear me?"

"Yes, Paige. I can hear you." Talking to drunk people is the worst.

"Not where Mom and Dad think I am, thasss for surreee. Am I right?"

"Where does Mom think you are?"

"She thinks I'm in my room."

Shit. This was not good. "Are you at a party?"

"Yeah. Cameron's parents are out of town and so I snuck out and got a ride from Aiden and Ryan."

I had no idea who these people were, but she was right. Mom and Dad would kill her if they knew she snuck out and went to a party with two guys and got drunk.

"Are they bringing you back home?"

"Thas the thing. They're passed out in the pool house. Thas why I called you."

On the one hand, I was irritated that she thought I was some kind of Uber or something. I live 25 miles away and it was the middle of the night. On the other hand, she called me instead of letting some drunk friend drive her home. This was what every big sister hopes will happen.

"You want a ride?"

"If it's okay. I mean, if you have a guy there or something..." She giggled as she said it.

"Very funny." I rubbed my eyes and yawned. It was going to be a long night. "Text me the address and I'll be there in about 40 minutes."

"Thanks, sis."

An hour later we were in my car. I'd had to go into some frat house down by Cal State Dominguez Hills and go inside to find her.

It was like some kind of horrible gauntlet of drunk college boys. "Hey there. What's your name?"

"My name is 'I'll kick you in the balls if you don't take that hand off my arm.'"

"Geez. You don't have to be like that."

The entire place smelled like cheap beer and weed. It reminded me of my college days, honestly. Empty pizza boxes all over the place. Red Solo cups. The party seemed to be winding down, but there were still probably 25 people hanging around, drunk and laughing and being obnoxious kids.

Finally, I found Bailey outside on a bench, looking like she was about to hurl. I was a combination of furious and relieved. This was no place for a sixteen-year-old girl. But the lectures could wait until tomorrow.

We got her things and made it down the hill to my Honda. As I was buckling her up, I noticed that she reeked of alcohol. There was no way Mom and Dad wouldn't notice. Hopefully the smell would dissipate before morning.

"Where are we going?" Bailey was in the passenger seat of the car and I was just praying she didn't puke in the ten minutes it would take to get her back home.

"Home. Where did you think we were going? Taco Bell?"

"I can't go home like this!" Bailey said. "They'll know I was drinking."

"Just sneak back in the way you snuck out."

"My room is on the second floor! I can't climb that tree." I knew from experience that she was right. It was much easier to sneak out of that house than to sneak back in. The house alarm would activate unless you left your window open a crack when Mom or Dad were setting it so it would bypass your room. Then, if you opened any other window or door, the alarm would sound.

"So what are we supposed to do, Bailey?" I was annoyed. It was late. I was tired. I just wanted to go home.

"Mom and Dad have tennis in the morning. Can I sleep at your place and then you bring me back while they're gone?"

Nothing like an extra fifty-mile trip. "Sure, Bailey. You can sleep on my couch."

Remind me never to have kids...

For a second, I forgot where I was. It was quiet and there were birds chirping and the gentle sound of an airplane flying overhead. The peace and calm reminded me of being home in Verde Hills. Until I heard a siren and remembered that I was in La Playa.

La Playa. Such a nice-sounding name for a shitty place to live. To be honest, not every place in the town was bad. There were some really nice areas near the university and the country club. But the areas that were bad were SO bad.

The memory of last night started to come back to me and I remembered that Bailey was here. We needed to get her back before Mom and Dad got back from tennis and then their weekly lunch with the Schweigers at the club. I would talk to her about making better choices on the way there.

Rolling out of bed, I grabbed my robe and yelled through the door, "Bail? Are you up yet?"

The apartment was silent, so she was probably still passed out. I opened my bedroom door and called her again. "Bailey. We need to get going if we're going to get you back home before Mom and Dad."

No response. "Bailey?"

She wasn't here! The blanket that she'd used was on the floor and the bathroom door was open, which meant she wasn't in there. That was all there was to this apartment. She was most definitely not here.

Where the hell could she have gone?

RYDER

I needed to stop by the shop to change the oil on my bike. Sunday was the best day to work on it because Ortega's Autos was closed and the regular guys were off riding or getting drunk or whatever the hell the other mechanics did on weekends.

Pulling up the driveway, I was relieved that no one was here. I'd just be able to get in, get the work done, and get back home in time for Cops.

I unlocked the thick padlock and dragged the heavy metal gate open. Ortega's Autos did auto repair on all kinds of cars, but we specialized in American makes. This wasn't the place to take your Porsche or Mercedes. It was where you went when your Chevy Cavalier needed a tune up and it was off warranty. Oh sure, we got the occasional T-bird or Camaro, but for the most part, this wasn't the place to bring your muscle car or your high-end auto. Padre wanted to fly under the radar, and so Ortega's was the kind of nondescript auto shop you'd see on street corners in every town.

My nose was hit with nostalgia as I walked in. The combination of motor oil, tire rubber, and electronic equipment reminded me of when I first started working here. I hadn't known a thing about cars, let alone bikes. This was the only job I'd ever had and I worked my way up from being an assistant mechanic to being the shop supervisor. The only one I answered to was Padre.

Twenty minutes later, I was finishing up my oil change when I heard Padre's bike rumble up. I would be glad to talk to him, since we hadn't really seen each other in awhile. He'd been acting so weird I figured maybe we could clear the air.

"Ryder," he said, as he came through the side door. "I'm glad you're here. We need to talk."

I'd wanted to talk, too, but there was something in his tone that told me this wasn't going to be a social conversation.

"Sure, I'll be right in." I wiped my hands off on a shop towel and put away the tools and then went over to the small office located at the back of the shop floor.

The door was closed so I knocked on the frosted window.

"Yeah," he said through the door.

I opened the door and went in. Figuring we were alone, I left the door open as I came inside.

"Close the door, Ryder."

Okay...not really sure why he wanted it closed, but I complied and then sat down on the bare metal folding chair opposite his desk.

The office looked like every shop owner's office. A metal file cabinet was stuffed in the corner, with auto supplies in boxes everywhere. Our license was in a cheap frame and hanging crookedly on the wall. Padre's desk was littered with invoices, bills, about a million pens, and a couple of half-drunk cups of coffee.

His tanned face had deepset lines and his brown eyes were starting to sink back in his face from age. He had salt-and-pepper hair that was thick and unruly, and broad, callused hands from a lifetime of manual labor. He was frowning and rubbing the back of his neck.

"Are you going to tell me what's going on, or am I going to have to ask?" He looked at me with those black eyes and there was no warmth or compassion coming from them at all.

I had no idea what he was talking about or why he was upset, but it was pretty clear he was. "I don't know what you mean, Padre."

"You don't?" he reached for a half empty bottle of water on his desk. "You don't have any idea why I would call you in here?" He took a swig and then licked his lips. "That's how you're going to play it?"

I wasn't "playing" anything, and if any other person on the planet talked to me like this I would already be up in his face. But this was Padre. "What's wrong, Padre?"

"What's WRONG, Ryder, is that you obviously thought I don't know what's going on around here and that you could get away with shit."

I shook my head, as I was at a total loss. "What are you talking about?"

"The parts? The missing parts that you're stealing from me. That's what I'm talking about."

I frowned and said, "Whoa! Padre! I'm not stealing anything. There are parts missing?" I was totally confused. I hadn't noticed anything missing at all. I had zero knowledge of any of this. "What's missing?"

Padre shook his head as if he didn't believe me. "I'm not going to tell you what I know because then you'll know what you got away with and what you didn't. I just wanted to warn you that I know what you're fucking doing and if it happens again you are going to be goddamn sorry. You remember what happened to Stryker."

Stryker was a patch who'd been taking cash under the

table for work he did for us and when Padre found out, he beat him so badly that the guy ended up in a wheelchair.

"Look, Padre. You know I wouldn't steal from you. You know me. If there are parts missing, let me—"

"I don't know shit, Ryder. You can't trust anyone a hundred percent. No one. The only reason I'm talkin' to you about this instead of kicking your ass first is because of our history. But that's done and now I'm warning you. Any more parts go missing around here and it's on you."

He glared at me with watery eyes and a stone-set jaw. The conversation was apparently over.

The chair scraped the floor as I stood up. "I'll find out who did it, Padre." Without another word, I left his office and shut the door behind me.

To say I was upset would be an understatement. I truly couldn't believe that Padre would accuse me of stealing from him. After everything that had happened between us! I thought of him like a father, and I thought he considered me a son.

As soon as I left the shop, I headed straight to the gym. I needed to get my head clear from all the shit going on. First, the trouble with Lily and Scorpion. Then there was Paige and how I found myself thinking about her all the time. And now this.

I always kept workout stuff in my bike bag and so I didn't need to stop. Swole gave me and the rest of the guys free memberships, although these days I was pretty much the only one who took advantage of it.

"Hey Ryder," she said as I walked in the gym. "Wasn't expecting you today."

Swole was our Sergeant at Arms. She was in charge of

security for the Outlaw Souls and she did a great job. She got the nickname "Swole" when she became a member because of her muscular physique. I didn't think she used steroids, but I couldn't be sure. Her biceps were bigger than mine, and when she was in a fight, she was like a ferocious dog that wouldn't stop until her opponent was unconscious and bleeding. You did not want to fuck with Swole.

I didn't want to talk, so I just nodded hello and headed to the locker room to change. My life might be spiraling out of control, but there were a few things I was still in charge of, and one of them was my body. I was going to run fast, lift hard, and force my body to remember who was boss. No more sexy dreams about Paige. No more feeling helpless with Lily or feeling betrayed by Padre. Just me, sweating until I couldn't think anymore.

PAIGE

As I pulled my car out of the parking space that I knew would be gone by the time I got back, I was a combination of angry, worried, and sad. I was angry because Bailey had just taken off without even thinking to leave me a note. I had no idea where she was, but I knew she couldn't get far on foot. La Playa was a big town inside an even bigger city.

I was worried about her on two levels. One, I was worried about what could happen to her in a town like this. A rich white girl walking around in last night's party clothes is an invitation for trouble. But on a deeper level, I was worried about her acting out like this. Sneaking out, getting drunk at a college party, and then not even thinking to tell me where she went this morning—that wasn't like Bailey.

The reason I was sad was that I saw so much of myself in her. We had the same judgmental parents who were as emotionally unavailable as they were critical. Unlike me, though, Bailey had an older sister who actually cared and was someone who would literally come to her rescue at one in the morning. Which led me back to being angry again.

Driving around on a Sunday morning, I tried to think of where she would go. Where would I have gone?

For one thing, she was likely to be hungover. I doubted she'd go to Tiny's and have a sit-down breakfast all by herself. It was more likely to be somewhere that she could go and grab something to eat or drink and get back to my apartment before I woke up. Which led to one place near here—the Southgate Martinez market.

Sure enough, just as I pulled into the parking lot, Bailey came walking out of the store, eating a burrito that was wrapped in tin foil. She had a horchata drink and a white plastic bag draped over her arm.

I pulled the Honda up and rolled down the passenger window. "Bailey!"

Her face lit up and she even had the nerve to smile. "Oh, hi Paige. Thanks for coming to get me." She pulled open the car door and got in the passenger side.

"'Hi, Paige'? That's what you have to say to me?" I was mad and not doing a very good job of containing it.

"Should I have said hola?" She took a big sip of her drink, grinning.

I sat there for a moment, contemplating my response. If I blew up at her now, there would be no chance of her listening to me about the bigger stuff I needed to say. So I just took a deep breath and exhaled and smiled back. "Yes. 'Hola, Paige' would have been more appropriate around here."

"How did you know where I was?"

"I just thought about where I would go for hangover food and realized this was the closest place." I pulled the car out into traffic and asked, "Since when do you drink horchata?"

"Oh, I met this girl at the market. She was wearing the same Twenty One Pilots shirt as me. I don't see a lot of those in Verde Hills."

"Speaking of which, did you leave anything at my place or can we go straight home before Mom and Dad get back?"

"No, we're good."

I turned the car in the direction of the freeway and listened to her talk before getting into the serious stuff. She reminded me of myself so much at sixteen. Half of her was innocent and naïve and the other half was rebellious and ready to take on the world.

As she talked about the girl she'd met and how they'd exchanged phone numbers and how Bailey realized that La Playa was a lot cooler than she thought it was going to be, I realized that I had my moment to interject.

"I'm glad you called me last night and came to spend the night. I think we should try and spend more time together."

"Seriously?" Bailey looked at me with surprise. "That would be so cool. I am so sick of the shit at school, Paige. Everyone is so fake. It's all about whose dad knows which celebrity and what kind of car you drive. It has nothing to do with the real world."

As we drove by the homeless people and their tents set up along the sidewalk, I had to admit I knew exactly what she meant. It was the exact same reason I'd started working at the free clinic. We led such a sheltered life in Verde Hills and I wanted to get out and see what the world was all about.

"You're right about that, Bailey. But the thing is, sneaking out and getting drunk at parties isn't the real world either." She shot me a look and I said, "Look, I get it. Living with Mom is enough to drive anyone to drink. Look at Dad. I'm just trying to help you avoid making my mistakes. There are plenty of ways for you to fuck up on your own. You don't have to steal mine."

She grinned and then I did, too. Bailey was a good kid, and she'd done the right thing by calling me to come get her last night. As concerned as I was about her, I knew that underneath it all, she had a good head on her shoulders.

As was typical for LA, we got stuck in traffic on the way up to Verde Hills. By the time we got there, it was past the time Mom and Dad should have been back. The mood in the car was tense as we turned on to our street. I was feeling more like I was the one who'd snuck out instead of the adult that I was.

"Shit. They're home." Bailey's voice sounded panicked. "What are we going to do?"

"I tell you what. I'll help you out this time and create a diversion, but you owe me a favor, okay?"

"What kind of favor?"

"I don't know yet. But when I need it, you have to do what I ask, no questions asked."

She looked back and forth between Dad's Audi and me. "Okay. Fine. What's the plan?"

"Paige? What are you doing here?" Mom looked surprised as I let myself in the kitchen door.

I didn't blame her for being surprised. I lived 25 miles away and wasn't famous for just "dropping by."

"Oh, I was in the neighborhood and figured I'd stop by and say hi." I went over to kiss her on the cheek as she was taking some French bread out of her fabric Farmer's Market bag.

"Oh! Well. That's...unexpected. I'm sure your dad and sister will be thrilled to see you."

As if on cue, Bailey came in from the back sliding glass door. "Oh hi, Paige! What are you doing here?"

Mom turned to look and was momentarily confused as to why Bailey was in the backyard, but then Bailey came and gave her a hug and said, "Is there a family meeting I didn't know about?"

Mom wrinkled her nose and said, "Have you been working in the garden or something? You smell like old fertilizer."

I had to stifle a laugh. What she really smelled like was stale beer.

"Who smells like old fertilizer?" Dad said as he came downstairs. "Oh, hi, Paige. What are you doing here?"

Bailey and I gave each other a side glance and I winked at her. Mission accomplished.

RYDER

I'd decided to stop off at the Blue Dog for a cup of coffee and one of their sandwiches for lunch before work. To say the Blue Dog was famous for food would be like saying that Kim Kardashian was famous for boxing. The sandwich was nothing more than a couple of pieces of white bread with some cold cuts they probably bought across the street at Southgate Martinez. Or maybe even brought from home.

But I was avoiding Tiny's because I didn't want to run into Paige. I was thinking about her more often than I wanted to already, and that was not good. I needed to stay sharp and not distracted. This stuff with Padre was really concerning, and I wondered if I was the only one who noticed the changes in him. He was never a warm, fuzzy guy, but there was a hardness now that I hadn't seen before.

A gust of fresh air blew through the place as the door opened. I could recognize the tall, thin frame of Hawk from the shadow he cast into the room. He was one of those "skinny muscle" guys and was built like a martial artist. Long, lean, and fast. There wasn't an ounce of fat on his body and he wore his thinning hair back in a long ponytail.

Padre had given him the nickname "Hawk" because he watched over everything and was able to get intel like no one else. He also got the nickname because his nose was big and curved, like a beak.

He saw me as he bellied up to the bar. "Whiskey, neat," he said to the bartender. Nodding in my direction, he said, "Ryder."

I grabbed my coffee cup, leaving the sandwich on the table I'd been sitting at, and went up to sit next to him. I was glad that the place was pretty empty because I wanted to pick his brain.

"Hey, Hawk. How's it going?"

"Pretty good. The old lady went to Pachanga with her sister for a coupla days so I'm batching it." He raised his glass and said, "Liquid lunch."

"So, Hawk. Have you noticed anything going on with Padre?"

His eyes narrowed a bit and I could tell that he knew something. "Whaddya mean?"

"Well, for starters, he's missed a couple times at church."

"So? Lotsa guys do that."

"True, but he's the President. But also, he's just been acting...I dunno, weird. Working odd hours. Seems distant."

Hawk didn't say anything and took a sip of his drink and set it down. There was a minute or so of silence as he was contemplating his response. Then he sighed and said, "Yeah. I noticed."

Relief washed over me. I didn't want to say anything about him accusing me of stealing if I didn't have to. I was just glad to know that I wasn't the only one who saw changes in Padre. "What do you think is going on?"

"Honestly, it reminds me of my dad before he got diagnosed with Alzheimers. The personality change was our first clue. He was acting kinda paranoid and suspicious."

That would make a lot of sense. My heart sank at the thought. What if Padre was having cognitive issues and this wasn't just some phase?

"Oh!" Hawk said. "I almost forgot. The guy I know over in Las Balas says that Scorpion is almost ready for his initiation. I figured I should let you know, since he's seeing Lily and all."

Shit. That was the last thing I needed right now. I shook my head and said, "Thanks, man. Not what I want to hear, but I'm glad you told me."

Hawk looked me in the eye and his small brown eyes carried a warning. "You need to do something about this, Ryder. I'd hate to see anything bad happen to Lily."

He was right. It was time to take matters into my own hands.

I finished my lunch and went to the shop for a few hours, but I was distracted. I couldn't stop thinking about what Hawk had told me about Scorpion. I needed to find that little shit and knock some sense into him, if need be. He needed to step away from my sister immediately.

"Chalupa," I called to him under the body of a car.

"Wassup, boss?"

"I'm taking off for a bit. You got things around here?"

"No prob. It's all good."

That was the thing. We had a loyal group of guys here at Ortega. Even if there were missing parts (which there weren't —I looked), no one would dare do that to Padre. We all knew what he was capable of. We were a team.

The afternoon sun was right in my face as I aimed my bike to downtown La Playa. Traffic was shit this time of day, so I took side streets. It was the reverse of what I'd done a few days ago... the graffiti and homeless encampments made way to million-dollar homes and art studios. It always shocked me how diverse La Playa was.

Las Balas used an old warehouse down by the pier to have their meetings and store their shit. La Playa had a huge port and commercial where boats and cruise ships would dock, and Las Balas took advantage of that to buy and sell shit illegally from the vessels before the Coast Guard got to them.

I got to the parking lot just as the sun set, locked my bike, and walked over to the warehouse. I wasn't expected, and I sure the hell wouldn't be welcomed. Some guys would call me crazy for just showing up like this, but I wanted the element of surprise.

I was taking a chance that Scorpion would even be there. As I walked up, I saw him outside guarding the door with another recruit, and they were both smoking cigarettes. That would explain why Lily smelled like a fucking ashtray sometimes.

His face was pockmarked from acne and his blond hair was swept back. He was not an attractive guy, not that I found guys attractive. I just couldn't imagine what the fuck Lily saw in this loser.

He must have sensed me because he looked up and then his body shot up in alarm. His hand went to his pocket, so I shouted, "Leave it, Scorpion. I just want to talk."

The other prospect ran off, ostensibly to alert the other guys, and so I knew I had about two minutes. Scorpion just stood there, frozen, looking from side to side.

"I got nothin' to say." His jaw was set defiantly, but I could tell from the way he bit his lip and his eyes darted back and forth that he was nervous.

"Good. Then listen." I got about four inches from his face. "You need to leave my sister the fuck alone."

"The fuck I do. She can make up her own mind."

I felt rage coil in my belly. This piece of shit kid was about to get seriously injured. "No, she cannot. She is a sixteen-year-old girl. You want to go to prison?"

At that, his body wilted and he looked at me. "Ryder. Give me a break, man. I love her."

That surprised me. "You love her? What the fuck does that even mean?"

"I do. I love her. She's beautiful, and smart, and funny..."

"And better than you in every goddamn way." I couldn't believe my ears. This guy actually thought he loved my sister?

He looked down at his feet. "I know."

I sighed. "Look. If you love her—which I doubt you actually do—then leave her the hell alone. This is no life for her. You know that."

He laughed sardonically, revealing yellow crooked teeth. "*You're* saying that?"

I grabbed him by the collar of his T-shirt. "My life and choices are none of your goddamn business. Let me put it another way. This is not a request, and I am not asking nicely. Leave my sister the hell alone or you will regret it every day for the rest of what's left of your short life. Got it?"

I could hear the rest of Las Balas coming, so I let him go and ran to my bike. Hopefully he got the message.

As I roared back to North La Playa, my mind started to wander to the place it seemed to go most these days: Paige. I needed to do something about it, but I wasn't sure what.

PAIGE

"Paige. What are you doing?" Martha was standing in the kitchen like a drill sergeant, barking orders at everyone. "Take this order to table four."

Table four wasn't my table, it was Rocky's, but I wasn't about to say that to Martha, so I grabbed the plates and headed over to deliver the food. Where was she? Rocky had just disappeared about an hour after I got to work.

I was exhausted. My neighbors had another booming party last night and the smell of weed came through the air conditioning vent so strongly that I actually felt high. I'd smoked a little pot in college, but I would prefer to be the one to choose it, not have it come through the vents. I just hoped this place didn't drug test.

"Excuse me, miss. This isn't syrup. It's soy sauce."

I looked at the glass container I'd put down next to the pancakes and sure enough, I'd grabbed the wrong thing. "Oh, I'm sorry. I'll be right back with your syrup."

Where was my head? Out of the corner of my eye, I could see the activity at the Blue Dog across the street. I found myself thinking about Ryder and wondering what he was up to. He hadn't come into Tiny's in a while and I was saving my money to move out, so I hadn't gone into the bar.

"Hello! Paige!" Martha was standing next to me, looking up and frowning. She was holding a bottle of syrup and I was still holding the soy sauce. "What is with you today?"

"Sorry, Martha, I'm just tired. I didn't sleep well, and with Rocky disappearing I've been covering her tables too. I'll do a better job of focusing."

"Who disappeared?" As if on cue, Rocky walked up behind me holding a couple of plates and setting them down at one of my tables. "If you need to go home, Paige, I can cover your tables."

I frowned. Part of what I was distracted from was covering for her for the last hour. "No, I'm good."

Martha stood looking back and forth between us. "Actually Paige, Rocky is right. Why don't you take off? Tomorrow is your day off. Come back rested and ready to work."

Before I had a chance to argue, Martha walked off to the kitchen. Rocky leaned over and whispered, "Next time you call me out like that, I'll get you fired. Martha listens to me."

She sashayed back into the kitchen, leaving me to wonder what the hell just happened.

I was kind of in a daze as I left work. I wasn't happy about being sent home, but on the other hand, I did need some time off. Maybe I'd call and see if I could reschedule that job interview. Working at Tiny's wasn't exactly my ultimate career ambition.

I was running a little low on gas, which is why I went to the gas station that was in the same parking lot as the Blue Dog. They had the best prices, I told myself. But the whole time I was pumping gas, I was scanning the parking lot. I couldn't admit it, but I was looking for his bike.

"Are you done?" A teenage boy was standing next to me and I became aware that I was still holding the gas dispenser even though my tank was full. His car was behind mine, waiting for the pump.

"What? Oh yeah. Sorry." I put the pump back and screwed on the gas cap. Just as I was getting the receipt, I heard it. The distinctive rumble of Ryder's bike.

My body jolted with electricity. There he was. Just on the other side of the parking lot. I saw him dismount his bike and take off his helmet. His long legs were clad in faded blue jeans that hugged every muscle. His jacket was faded from exposure to the elements.

"Are you going to be leaving soon, or should I move to another pump?" The guy behind me was irritated and I didn't blame him a bit. I was acting like a moron.

"No, I'm sorry. I'm going."

As if it had a mind of its own, my car made its way across the parking lot to the Blue Dog. "I'll just get a Diet Coke," my mind said, but it was a lie. I knew why I was going in there.

The smell of Lysol, stale beer, and cigarettes hit my nose at the same time my eyes went blind from the change to darkness. I felt really out of place in my sensible waitress shoes and my Tiny's T-shirt. I half-expected them to hand me a tray and tell me to start taking orders.

My eyes adjusted and I saw Ryder leaning over the jukebox. It was like that Taylor Swift song—he was looking like James Dean in those jeans and leather jacket.

A magnetic attraction pulled me to where he was. I had no idea what I was going to say, but I just knew I needed to be near him.

"Hey." *That was brilliant, Paige. Did they teach you that in college?*

"Oh! Paige! I didn't expect to see you here. What are you doing here?" It might have been my imagination or all the weed I didn't smoke last night, but he seemed to be happy to see me.

"Don't choose that song," I said.

"Why not?" he asked.

"Because if we end up getting married and living happily ever after, I don't want Tequila to be our song." Who was this bold woman speaking from my mouth?

"Our song?" he laughed and asked, "Okay. What should I pick, then?"

I leaned over the jukebox and could feel his gaze going up and down my body, lingering on my ass. "What about this one?" I said, pointing to a title.

"Born to be Wild? You want our kids to play that at every anniversary?"

"Okay, how about this?" I pointed to Patsy Cline's *Anything.* The way he was looking at me, he could have done anything to me and I'd have agreed.

Without a word, he pushed the numbers on the jukebox and walked over to the bar. The bartender slid over a cup of coffee. I followed him like a puppy.

"Can I get a Diet Coke?" I asked her.

"That shit'll kill you," Ryder said, grinning at me.

"So can riding a bike," I said.

"If you don't know how to handle it."

"And you do?" I said, looking up at him. "You know how to handle it?"

The smile spread across his face slowly, revealing deep dimples. "Honey, you have no idea."

He took his coffee over to a table in the back and the

waitress gave me my Diet Coke. I grabbed for my wallet, but Ryder said, "Put it on my tab."

This was the second time someone had bought my drink here. I grabbed the glass and went over to Ryder's table. "Thanks."

"It's the least I could do," he said, motioning for me to sit down.

"Why is that?"

"You saved me from telling an embarrassing story for the rest of my life. Imagine explaining that Tequila was our song when I don't even drink."

"You don't?" That surprised me.

"Nope. Never touch the stuff."

I wanted to know why, but figured it was a topic of conversation for a different day, so I just took a sip of my Diet Coke.

"How's the job?" he asked, staring at the word Tiny's on my shirt.

My nipples must have sensed it because they instantly got hard. "It's okay. They sent me home early today." Why did I tell him that?

"Let me guess. Rocky went missing for an hour, you got stuck with her tables, and then when you messed up, Martha sent you home instead of her."

The shock must have registered on my face. "How did you know?"

"Let's just say it isn't the first time it's happened. Rocky has been there for years, and I don't know what the loyalty thing is, but it's real."

"I had no idea." The soda had gone to my bladder already, so I looked around. "Where are the restrooms?"

"Back there." He nodded to the rear of the bar. "You go and I'll pick out another song."

"No Taylor Swift."

"Are you always this controlling?" he said.

"Only if you know how to handle it," I said as I walked down the hall. My boldness was shocking even to myself.

He was waiting for me as soon as I came out of the bathroom. I could hear the strains of some bluesy song on the jukebox as I looked up at him. The hall was slightly dark, and a lock of his hair fell forward onto his forehead as he leaned one arm over my head against the wall.

I opened my mouth to say something witty, but his lips came down on mine before I got the chance. He tasted like black coffee and gum. He was surprisingly gentle at first. Soft kisses on my lips.

The passion that had been building between us since the first moment we met ignited and we soon became a tangle of arms and hands, bodies pressing against each other, tongues exploring.

My mind shut off and my body took over. I wanted more. I was hungry for him and wanted him to fill every inch of me, deeply and completely.

"Hey, can I get in here?" Some girl was standing next to us, trying to get into the bathroom.

"Oh, sorry." I turned around to let her in the door and by the time I turned back, Ryder was gone.

My heart was pounding and my lips were bruised from his kisses. I thought about chasing after him but realized that this was for the best. I needed to clear my head before this whole thing went too far.

Maybe it already had.

RYDER

I slipped out the back door as fast as possible. I was on the verge of making a huge mistake with Paige and needed to stop the damage before it went too far.

Who was I kidding? It had already gone too far. My bike roared to life and I headed down Berry Avenue. I didn't know where I was going, but I knew I needed to get the hell out of there.

What was with that woman? Why couldn't I stop thinking about her? Wanting to touch her? Even worse... wanting to talk to her?

This was not good. I was a single "parent" for all intents and purposes, and the crap with Lily and Scorpion was what needed to be my focus.

Unless she was at the age where she needed a woman in her life to talk to...

No. No. That was bullshit. Maybe I was just horny. If I just got laid, maybe I could get back to focusing on my real life and not that blonde with the blue eyes and the cherry lips that had wandered into my life.

Banking my bike to the right, my mind was made up. I

knew what I needed to do, and I knew exactly who to go to and do it with.

"Hey, sexy. Long time no see." Sofia was leaning up against the door of her mobile home wearing not much more than a slip. It was a white cotton dress and it clung to every one of the curves I knew so well. "I was real happy to get your text." She stepped aside. "Come on in."

As I went into the small home, it looked exactly the same as it had the first time I was here. Sofia was really into Latin art, and her whole place looked like a huge Dia De Los Muertos exhibit. Colorful skulls, half-burned candles, and paintings everywhere.

Padre had given me Sofia's address when I was 18. He said it was time I learned a few things. I wasn't a virgin, of course. But Sofia knew a whole lot more about sex than my high school girlfriend had.

Sofia wasn't a professional or anything. She was just a good friend to Padre and was willing to help him out with just about anything.

"Can I get you a beer, or are you still not drinkin'?" She crossed over to the small refrigerator.

"No, I'm good, thanks."

"Mind if I have one?" she asked.

"Knock yourself out." I went to sit on the couch. Oddly, I felt awkward. I hadn't been here in a good year, year and a half. Sofia and I had played around quite a few times, but it was never anything serious.

"So what's on your mind, Ryder?" She sat down across from me and looked at me with tender brown eyes.

I tried to play it cool. "Does a guy have to have something on his mind to come see an old friend?"

"You do." She crossed her tanned legs and for a moment I wished we weren't having this conversation. I wished I had those legs wrapped around my waist and I could stop thinking about the reason I was here. "You don't just come by, Ryder."

I didn't know how to answer that, so I didn't. I just shifted in my seat.

Suddenly, her face broke out in a smile. "It's a woman! You're here because of a woman."

I shook my head, not in disagreement but in disbelief. "How could you tell?"

"Ryder, I've known you since you were just becoming a man." She took a sip of her beer. "Who is she?"

"She's a new waitress at Tiny's." It felt weird even talking about Paige with her. Or anyone, for that matter.

"And you like her?"

"I don't know what I feel." I kept looking at Sofia and trying to find a way to stop the conversation and just get her in bed. I wanted to not think or feel or do anything for a while.

Sofia got up, crossed over to where I was, and kneeled down in front of me. I could see down her dress, and for a moment thought she was making a move. Instead, she took both of my hands in hers and said, "Can I give you some advice?"

"Sure."

"The biggest regret in my life is not going after love when it showed up on my doorstep. I was too afraid to open up and risk getting hurt. Instead, I ran so fast the other way my head was practically spinning. Eventually he left and married someone else, and here I am, alone."

It was at that moment that I truly looked at Sofia for the first time. Not as a person who was there to teach and comfort me, but as a person. She had feelings and a heart and was a woman, not just some receptacle to take away my pain. I knew that she deserved better than that.

"Sofia..."

She quickly stood up and went to grab her beer. "Don't feel sorry for me, Ryder. But don't become me, either. If you have any feelings toward this woman at all, follow them. Sure, you might get hurt, but at least you won't spend the rest of your life wondering if it could have turned out differently."

I stood up because it was time for me to leave. "Thank you, Sofia." I hugged her warmly. "I really appreciate what you said."

"You take care of yourself, Ryder."

Fifteen minutes later I was headed back to North La Playa. It was a good thing I was such a seasoned rider, because my head was completely in the clouds and I'd have been a danger to myself if it weren't so instinctive.

I couldn't stop thinking about what Sofia had said about Paige. What if it were time to take a chance again? I mean, I wasn't planning on being alone forever. Maybe it would be good for Lily if I had a woman around for her to look up to. Not just some biker chick but an actual lady.

I'd made up my mind to find Paige and see if she wanted to have dinner or something when I felt my phone buzz with a text message. At a stoplight, I took my phone out and read it. It was Chalupa.

U need to get to the shop ASAP. Padre is losing it.

All thoughts of Paige, Lily, and Sofia left my mind in an instant. First and foremost, I was a member of Outlaw Souls. We were brothers, and if one of us needed help, that was all that mattered. My reply was simple.

On my way.

PAIGE

I was digging through a box looking for the blouse my mother gave me last year for Christmas. I hadn't fully unpacked since moving in, and really didn't go out to the kinds of places where you had to dress up.

As I was throwing the contents of the box onto the bed, my mind started to wander to that makeout session with Ryder. What the hell was I going to do about him? Rocky had said he was bad news, and the last thing I needed was to get emotionally involved with some biker.

Sure, Rocky wasn't the most reliable source on the planet, and Ryder didn't seem like just "some biker." He was smart and funny and seemed like a really nice person.

A really nice person who does all kinds of illegal stuff, Paige. You need to stay away.

But as many times as I told myself to leave it alone, I always found myself wanting more.

"Found it!" I grabbed the cobalt blue top and took it into the bathroom. I was meeting my parents and Bailey for dinner up in Verde Hills to celebrate my mom's birthday. I hadn't seen them since that day with Bailey and I was definitely not looking forward to the judgmental questions that were sure to come.

"Things are going great, Mom and Dad. I got sent home from my waitress job after I tried to serve soy sauce with pancakes because I was thinking about this hot biker. Oh, and I ended up making out with him later that day." I grinned at myself in the mirror, imagining the conversation. "The apartment? Oh yeah, it's fabulous. It's like a combination dispensary and night club. But at least the prostitutes are quieter than the sorority girls who come to party."

Part of me wondered if I shouldn't just pack up and go home. I fluffed up my hair, smacked my lips to distribute my lipstick, and grabbed my purse. I had to get to the club by seven, and LA traffic is the pits.

***

"You're late." My mother was sitting in her usual spot at our usual table at the Los Verdes Country Club. The clock over the bar said 7:07 pm.

I went over and kissed her on the cheek, getting a whiff of her martini. "I'm sorry, Mom. The freeway was a mess."

"You wouldn't need to take the freeway if you didn't live in that place."

"Give her a break, Mom. She lived on campus at SC. You act like she never left home before." Bailey was having what appeared to be a sparkling water. My guess, though, was that she'd spiked it with some vodka when Mom and Dad weren't looking. She learned that little trick from me.

I pulled the chair out and slid in between my parents. I kissed my dad on the cheek and put my napkin on my lap just as Miranda came up.

"Good to see you, Paige. Can I get you started with a drink?"

I ordered a glass of wine and then asked my mom about tennis, what was new with her friends, and other small chit chat. The whole thing took about ten minutes and then I was out of things to say.

This was going to be a long-ass dinner.

I had a mouthful of linguini carbonara when it happened. Honestly, I was surprised it took so long.

"So, Paige." My dad cleared his throat. "How is your little adventure going? Have you found a job saving the world yet?" He had the audacity to chuckle at his perceived wittiness.

My mother wiped her mouth and set her napkin down before getting up. "Excuse me a moment." She then went in the direction of the ladies' room.

"What's with her?" I asked, hoping to change the conversation.

"You know that she's not happy about your life choices, Paige."

I swear these people must live in a bubble. My "life choices" were moving to a disadvantaged neighborhood and trying to find some way to help. It's not like I joined a gang.

Imagine if they knew about Ryder...

I took a sip of wine and said, "As a matter of fact, things are going great. I had an interview with the Californians for Social Justice." It was true. I did have an interview. Scheduled. That I missed. I made a mental note to call Elizabeth Maroni again tomorrow.

His eyebrows went up in surprise. "Oh really? I've never heard of them. Who heads them up?"

I didn't want to get into it, and fortunately my mother came back and saved me by changing the subject.

"I ran into Gladys Weinstein in the bathroom. That

woman had another face lift! Her face is already so lifted she could reach the space station."

My dad chuckled and Bailey and I shot each other a glance.

"Your sister tells me that you and she are going to a concert together?" My mom held her martini glass up to indicate to Miranda that she was ready for another.

I knew nothing about this and glared at Bailey. "Uhhh, yeah!"

Bailey jumped in. "Yeah! My favorite band, My Chemical Romance, has finally gotten back together for a reunion tour, and they're playing at the La Playa Convention Center of all places. You remember we saw Gerard Way a few years ago, but this is the whole band!"

"What a stupid name for a group," was all our mother said as Miranda set her third martini down in front of her.

"Well, you girls have fun, but be safe. You know better than anyone what that neighborhood is like, Paige," Dad said.

"Actually, the convention center is in a really nice neighborhood." Not like where I lived, I thought.

The whole time we were having this conversation, I was shooting daggers from my eyes at Bailey. I hoped she didn't really expect me to go sit through some concert with her.

"Let's hit the little girls' room, Bail." I stood up and she sheepishly did too.

"What the hell was that?" We were washing our hands in the marble sinks.

"Sorry, Paige. I thought I texted you. I'm going to the concert with that chick I met at the market the day I stayed with you."

I figured I'd better check my texts and see if maybe she

did text me. I'd been a little distracted lately. "That chick you met?"

"Yeah. Lily?"

I scanned my mind and vaguely remembered her telling me about it. "Oh yeah."

"She's great. Totally real and normal. Gets good grades and everything."

"Why not tell Mom and Dad the truth?" As soon as I asked the question, I knew the answer. If she didn't live in Verde Hills, my parents would think she wasn't good enough to be friends with their precious daughter. They were so elitist!

"You know why. Anyway, I thought I could just spend the night after. If that's okay."

I was reapplying my lipstick and said, "Sure, that's fine. Maybe we can get dinner before the concert or something. Does she drive?"

"I don't think so. She's sixteen but hasn't gotten her license yet. We talked about doing it together."

We headed out to the dining room and I said, "Sounds good, Bailey. Just make sure I know about this kind of stuff before I hear about it from Mom and Dad."

She hugged me and said, "Thanks, Paige. You're the best."

RYDER

I could hear the shouting and things crashing as soon as I turned off my bike. I locked it (never forget to do that) and ran to the door.

"I'm not goddamn kidding, Chalupa. Shit is missing and I'm not gonna stop until I find it."

I heard a huge crash and some glass shatter. "Padre, stop! There's nothing missing! I took inventory myself." Chalupa sounded desperate.

"Padre." I used my most commanding voice. "What is going on?"

The man that looked back at me was not the man I knew. His hair was wild and out of control and his dark eyes showed panic. The shop was completely trashed, with tool cabinets dumped out and shattered glass everywhere. At least the customers' cars seemed to be untouched.

I went over to him and grabbed his arm, gently but firmly. "Padre. Let's go into your office and talk it through."

"You think I'm going to trust you?" he said.

"Padre. Ryder just wants to talk." Chalupa stood there running his hands through his hair.

At that moment, Swole walked in, and behind her was Moves. Our private security team. "Padre. Listen to them. You need to stop."

"The fuck I do. This is MY shop and I'll be damned if people are stealing from me." Padre lunged for another tool box and Swole and Moves rushed to grab him and pin him back.

It wasn't until Yoda came in the back door that Padre stopped struggling. "Paul," he said, using Padre's given name. "Let's go for a walk."

He nodded to me to come and to Swole and Moves to let him go. Yoda walked to the door and said, "Come on. The fresh air will do you good."

<hr />

The day was warm and sunny, and if you didn't know what had just gone down it would seem like another perfect day in Southern California.

I stayed a few paces behind, close enough that I could hear what was being said, but far enough that they could talk just the two of them. We walked down Berry Avenue in the direction away from the Blue Dog.

"What's going on, Paul?"

"My people are stealing from me, Ming." His voice sounded gravelly and upset.

'How do you know?"

"Things aren't where I left them. I go to look for a tool and it's not there."

"Have you talked to the guys about it?" His tone was compassionate.

"I did, but they just lie about it. I won't tolerate this kind of thing, Yoda. You know that."

"Of course. Can I ask why they would steal from you?

You've been nothing but loyal to everyone at Ortega and Outlaw Souls."

"I know. That's the thing. I just can't believe it."

"Is it possible you're mistaken?"

He stopped and looked at Yoda, totally unaware that I was there. I stopped, too.

"It is possible. I've noticed some...changes."

"What kind of changes?"

"In me. In my mind and my memory and stuff. I get so mad. Just explosive rage over stupid shit. I turned my television upside down when some guy won on Wheel of Fortune when he shouldn't have."

"Have you been to a doctor?" Yoda started walking again, slowly, and Padre and I did too.

Padre shook his head. "No. I don't wanna know. My mom lost her mind and I don't want it to happen to me."

"Paul. There are all kinds of medications and things nowadays. You can slow the progress, even if you can't stop it. Not finding out isn't going to make it better."

I couldn't believe my ears. I knew something was up with Padre. I just hoped he'd get help before someone got really hurt.

"Where is he now?" Pin was sitting to my left. "We don't want him walkin' in."

I'd called an emergency meeting of the Outlaw Souls, and we were in the back room of the Blue Dog. Everyone was here except for Padre, because he was the subject of the meeting.

I had the two prospects Kimberly and Carlos outside guarding the door, and we had a signal for if Padre walked into the bar. I didn't think he would be there, honestly. He'd had a rough day.

"I think he went home. We cleaned up the shop and it was a lot of physical labor. He's gotta be tired."

"So what are we gonna do about Padre?" Hawk asked. "We can't have a president who loses control like that."

"I know. It's a tough situation. I think we have some time, though, before we have to confront it directly. He promised Yoda he'd see a doctor and we have the Vegas run coming up. Plus, we're doing security for that concert down at the convention center next week. We have a lot to keep him busy with. Let's just make sure that one of us is always with him, except for when he's at home. This way if he starts thinking crazy shit, we'll be able to talk to him. Or at least alert each other."

It was a temporary solution and one that I hoped would work. Time would tell.

PAIGE

My alarm went off, and for a moment I had a sinking feeling of dread. Another day waiting tables at Tiny's.

It wasn't that I hated the job. It was honest work, the customers tipped well (although not as well as the ones Rocky got for letting them grab her ass), and it wasn't exactly hard. I just felt I was wasting my passion taking orders for today's special and lemon pie. As much as I hated to admit it, my parents were right: I didn't get a degree from USC to be waiting tables at a diner in North La Playa.

Almost as soon as the dread set in, though, it lifted as I remembered. My alarm wasn't for work, it was for a job interview!

A couple of days ago, Rocky asked if she could pick up a couple of extra shifts. She wanted to save up for concert tickets and needed the extra money. I called Elizabeth Maroni at the Californians for Social Justice job and finally rescheduled that interview and got Rocky to cover my shift. It was some kind of miracle that the position was still open and that Elizabeth was willing to still consider me after my missing the interview with no warning.

I practically leapt out of bed. Even the mess of Banner Manor couldn't ruin my mood today! It took just a few minutes to shower, fix my hair and makeup, and put on my interview outfit. I'd already stopped by FedEx Kinkos last night to print out my resume, and so I downed some coffee (being really careful not to spill!) and headed out the door.

The office was in downtown La Playa, not far from city hall and the convention center. As was typical for La Playa, traffic was a mess this time of day. But I didn't care. I was interviewing for a job!

By the time I finally got to the building (GPS took me to the wrong place), the regular parking lot was full and I had to pay $20 to park three blocks away in one of those valet lots. It was a warm morning and I wasn't exactly thrilled about having to walk that far in my heels right before a job interview. But what else could I do?

The sun was shining and there were seagulls cawing as the ocean breeze took a bit of the warmth off my face. If I got the job, this would be my workplace every day. That would be a Subway sandwich place I could go to at lunch. There would be my new Starbucks.

I really wanted this job.

The sign over the doors that said "Californians for Social Justice" was small. It was clearly not a big-budget place. I didn't care. It was better than Tiny's.

I pushed open the glass door and went inside. There was a small reception desk, but no one was at it. The walls of the waiting room were covered in posters about making a difference in the community. There were old magazines strewn about and a few metal chairs lined up against the wall.

I wasn't sure what to do since no one was at the desk, so I stood there for a few moments. When no one came out, I said, "Hello?"

No one answered and so I said it again. "Hello?"

I looked at my phone to see if maybe Elizabeth had called or texted to reschedule. Nothing. Maybe this was her way of getting even with me for standing her up? I doubted she would be that childish.

So I just stood there, looking around, wondering what to do.

Finally, a small woman holding a plastic box full of papers came walking in the room backwards. Her brown hair was in a braid and she was wearing a long denim skirt with flats. She appeared to be struggling with the box, so I said, "Here. Let me help you," and started to walk over to her.

Evidently I must have startled her because she jumped and said, "Oh!" and then dropped the box, spilling the papers.

"I'm sorry," we both said at the same time.

"I didn't hear you come in," she said.

"Yeah, I called out but no one was here."

"I was in the back getting these..." She spread her hands out and looked at the floor. She then looked up at me. "I assume you're Paige Anton?"

I nodded. "I am. Can I help you clean this up?" It was a rhetorical question as I bent down and started grabbing papers.

"These are all our old rejected grant applications for the past five years. We're in the process of re-applying and wanted to pull some information off of them." She looked at me. "You don't have any experience in grants, do you?"

I shook my head. "Not really. I'm a fast learner, though."

"No, we need someone who has experience getting grants. Our funding is running out and we need to source additional grants if we're going to stay afloat."

We finished putting the papers back in the box and she turned and started walking away. Was that it? The whole interview?

She then turned to look at me and said, "Come on. Follow me back here."

I did as instructed and followed her down a small hallway that led to a room that looked like it used to be a single office. There were four cubicles stuffed in it, one on each wall. It was insanely cramped and not at all what I'd been expecting.

"What did you get your degree in?" she asked, setting the box down on top of several others just like it.

"Sociology. My GPA was..."

"Too bad. We really need someone with a business background. Everyone on staff has a MSW."

That was the exact degree I'd been thinking of getting. But maybe a masters in social work wasn't such a good idea after all.

"Okay, so no grant experience. No business background. Do you know anything about fund raising? Or accounting?"

"I took an accounting class one summer in high school." This was not going very well, I could tell.

"I seem to recall reading that you grew up in Verde Hills. Do you have any contacts up there that might be a potential donor?"

Honestly, even if I did, I wasn't exactly going to call them and hit them up for money. I got that this place seemed to be hard up for funds, but I wanted to make a difference in the community, not raise funds for some organization. My goal was to work hands-on with young people.

I was starting to think that maybe this wasn't the job for me after all.

"No, I'm afraid I don't."

Elizabeth stood up and we both realized that the interview was over. "Well, Paige, as you can see we are really short-staffed and we need to find someone who can help get us the funding to stay afloat. We would welcome you as a volunteer, but..."

I smiled and extended my hand to shake hers. "Thank you for the interview and the opportunity, but I think I'll keep looking."

She nodded in understanding. "All right, then. Best of luck to you, Paige."

The smile faded as soon as I turned my back to walk out the door. Tears threatened to come and my heart sank. Maybe I should just quit and go home to Verde Hills. Maybe my parents were right, and this whole thing was a huge mistake.

RYDER

The church clock was gonging, telling me it was midnight. The church down the street from our apartment complex had this bell that went off every half hour. It was supposed to stop at night so nearby residents could get some sleep, but evidently the timer was broken so it gonged every half hour all day and night. While most people would find it irritating, I found it kind of soothing. Sort of a reminder that we were being watched over by a higher power.

But tonight I wasn't thinking about that or feeling soothed. Seething was more like it. Lily had said she and a friend from school were going to a movie that was supposed to get out at ten. The theater was literally three miles from here, so either they went somewhere else after, didn't go to the movie at all, or she was out with Scorpion again.

If it were the latter, that little shit better realize how close he was to being seriously injured by me. I was not kidding when I told him to leave Lily alone.

I stretched and then got up off the couch to turn the TV off. I knew I wouldn't be able to sleep until she got home, but I was sick of just sitting there waiting.

I went to the fridge to get a bottle of water when I heard her key in the door. That familiar feeling of relief and rage surged again. I just turned around and waited.

"Oh! Ryder. I didn't think you'd still be up." She came in but didn't meet my eye as she put her keys in the bowl.

One whiff of her told me she'd been with Scorpion. Not too many sixteen-year-old girls were chain smokers.

"You know I can't sleep when you're out. You're late."

"Oh, yeah. Hannah and I went to Baskin Robbins to get some ice cream after the movie."

She was lying straight to my face!

"I see." I turned my back and went to put the bottle in the recycling. "How was the movie?"

"Oh, it was good."

"Did the dog die in the end?" I knew the answer to this question because I'd accidentally read a spoiler about it online.

"Thank goodness, no. You know I hate movies where the dog dies."

I had her. "That's bullshit, Lily. And you know what's worse? You're lying straight to my fucking face. You know I hate it when people lie to me." My heart was pounding in anger.

"I'm not lying to you, Ryder. Why would you accuse me of that?"

Now she was lying to me about lying. But I could tell by the look on her face that she knew I'd caught her.

"You are really off track, Lily. You're hanging around that asshole and you're going to get hurt."

"If you're referring to Scorpion—who I was not with tonight, by the way—he is not an asshole. He loves me. And if you would just take the time to get to know him before you judged him—"

"Oh I know him, all right. I was him. You think I don't

see the hickeys on your neck? It's you who doesn't know him, Lily." I rubbed my face in exasperation. "Maybe we should just leave La Playa. Go somewhere where you can find people your own age to hang around with."

"I do have a friend my age. We're going to a concert together. The one at the convention center? She got tickets and invited me."

She was crazy if she thought I was going to believe her at this point. "What friend?" Those tickets were expensive. No one around here would be able to afford them, unless they were not a teenage girl or were into some illegal shit.

"Her name is Bailey. She doesn't live around here. We met at Southgate one day and started texting. She's really cool, Ryder. Not like the jealous bitches that go to my school."

That actually sounded believable. "The only way you're going to that concert, Lily, is if I drop you off and pick you up. With your new friend."

"Fine. I want you to meet her anyway. She was saying something about getting dinner first. Maybe you could come?"

For a moment Lily looked like a hopeful young girl. It was the way she'd looked before the accident.

"Okay," I said. "But let's go somewhere other than Tiny's." I did not want to risk running into Paige.

PAIGE

It had been a rough week, and I was ready for it to be over. After things went downhill with that job interview, I'd gotten really discouraged. I'd gotten crappy tips at Tiny's, dealt with loud neighbors smoking weed day and night, and couldn't stop thinking about Ryder. I didn't really have a reason to be avoiding him, but I felt like such a loser at the moment that I wasn't up for starting anything with someone. I needed to figure out my life first.

Which is why the timing of this concert for Bailey was so unfortunate. I had to drive all the way up to Verde Hills in the pouring rain, deal with my parents and the third degree, then drive all the way back to La Playa and have dinner with Bailey's new friend and her brother of all people. How I'd gotten roped into dinner with some girl and her pimply-faced brother, I did not know.

I figured I'd just drop them off at the concert, and she said the brother was going to give them a ride back here.

I checked myself in the mirror before heading out the door. I'd taken a nap after work and didn't bother to brush my hair, so I stuck it up in a messy bun. I wasn't going to bother with makeup either, since I really didn't care what Bailey's friends thought of my appearance. My parents would probably judge me, but they would do that no matter what. I threw on a Victoria's Secret PINK tracksuit and headed out the door.

Whoever said it doesn't rain in California has obviously never been here during an El Nino year. It wasn't just raining, there was water slamming out of the sky. I was actually sorry I'd given my umbrella to that homeless guy at the bus stop. Okay, no I wasn't, but I was sorry I hadn't replaced it.

Street parking was a disaster on rainy days and I had to park two blocks away, which meant that I was completely drenched by the time I got to the car. "You owe me big time, Bailey," I muttered under my breath.

"So. How's life treating you, Paige?" My mother sat at the kitchen island drinking a cup of tea.

It was pretty obvious from my damp clothes and hair and the scowl on my face that life was not treating me well at the moment. But I forced a smile on my face and said, "Things are great, Mom. Thanks for asking."

I glared at the stairs. What was taking Bailey so long? We weren't going to prom together. It was a concert.

"Any luck on the job search?" Mom asked.

I did not want to talk about this, so I just said, "Yes. I have a few leads." I then looked at my phone and yelled at the stairs. "Come *on*, Bailey. Traffic is bad because of the rain."

I didn't really care about being late for dinner, but I wanted to get away from my mother's inane questions.

Finally, I heard her clomping down the stairs. I was

surprised. She wasn't wearing a stitch of makeup, and had on a pair of sweats and a hoodie. This was what I'd been waiting for? An overstuffed backpack completed the ensemble. Frankly, she looked more like she was going camping for the weekend than to a concert.

I didn't care. I just wanted to leave. "Do you have everything??"

"I think so. Let's bounce."

I was so ready to bounce I could have tried out for the Lakers.

We were pulling out of the driveway and I could barely see a thing through the rain. "You were smart to wear a hoodie. This weather is crazy."

Bailey just grinned at me and pulled the hoodie over her head, revealing a skimpy tank top. Of course. Why hadn't I seen that coming? The old "cover up for the parents" trick. My guess was that she had a miniskirt under the sweats and makeup in the backpack.

"So where are we meeting these people for dinner?"

"It's this Italian place on Third Street. La Passarella. Lily says it's one of her favorite places in town."

Great. Just my luck. The pimply-faced kid wants somewhere nice and I'm dressed for a night out at Chipotle. Since when do kids eat at fancy Italian places?

"When you're done with that eyeliner, can you enter the address into the GPS?" I could barely see the cars in front of me because of the crazy rain. At least one of us would look good tonight.

Forty-five minutes of bumper-to-bumper traffic later, we were on Third Street. We were twenty minutes late for dinner and I couldn't find parking. "Why don't you get out and meet them and I'll park the car?"

I had to admit, Bailey looked gorgeous. Her blond hair was down and brushed, her makeup was gorgeous, and she looked happier than I'd seen her in a long time. Whoever this new friend was, she was having a positive influence on Bailey.

"She's just so real, Paige," she'd said on the drive over. "She hasn't had an easy life. Her parents were killed in a car accident but she's keeping it together. She's dating this older guy and even though he says he loves her and all, she's waiting until they move in together to have sex. She says she wants to make sure the guy means it."

I wasn't sure how to respond. How old was the guy? Was having sex at sixteen so common? Did this mean Bailey wasn't a virgin? There were too many questions, so I said, "Sounds like she's got a good head on her shoulders."

Now, as she slammed the car door shut and ran into the restaurant, I realized that she was closer to being a woman than she was to being a girl. When did that happen?

I got completely drenched again from the car to the door of La Passarelli. Everyone else had umbrellas and raincoats and I looked like something that had washed ashore.

Whatever. I'd have some dinner, drop the kids off at the convention center, and go home.

The smell of garlic bread hit my nose as soon as I walked in the place, making me realize that I was starving. I hadn't had a decent meal out since I moved to La Playa. This was the kind of restaurant I went to all the time in Verde Hills. Upscale, with a warm family vibe.

"Welcome to La Passarelli. I'm Lisa, the owner. Table for one?"

The place was packed. Photos of Lisa and a woman who appeared to be her mother were on the walls, along with other family photos. Frank Sinatra crooned softly on the radio, and each table was filled with happy, laughing people enjoying family style meals. Red and white checkered tablecloths and green ivy completed the scene.

"Actually, my sister just came in. She was meeting some friends?" I started to scan the room for Bailey and the pimply-faced kid and his sister.

"Oh! Of course. I should have known. She looks just like you. Follow me this way."

As I watched her walk ahead of me, I wondered how Lisa spent every night in those high heels. Her feet must have been a mess.

We walked around tables and squeezed through tight corners. I saw Bailey sitting next to a dark-haired girl and a guy with brown hair, who had his back to me.

"They're right over there," Lisa said. "Your server will be with you shortly."

There was something strangely familiar about the brother. I couldn't see his face, so it must have been something in his body language or demeanor.

Honestly, he reminded me a little bit of...

And then he turned around. "Ryder?"

"Paige?"

Of course. Of course I would run into him looking like this. Between the wet sweatsuit I was wearing, my ridiculous hair, and no makeup, I looked like I'd just come out of the ocean sporting a terrible hangover.

Ryder, on the other hand, looked so sexy I could die. He wasn't wearing his jacket, but instead had on this black Polo shirt that hugged his biceps. I wondered how often he got to the gym, because guns like that don't grow on their own.

I couldn't see under the table to see his pants, but he had a five o' clock shadow thing going on that made me instantly wet. I wanted to rub that beard all over my—

"What are you doing here?"

RYDER

I hated to admit it, but Lily's friend Bailey was nice. She seemed intelligent and had a lot more class than most of the other girls I'd seen Lily hanging out with. Pretty, blond, and you could tell she came from a good family with a lot of money. I was glad they'd met, although I'd never gotten the full story of how it happened that Bailey was at some random Mexican market in North La Playa.

Looking around the cozy restaurant, I was glad that Lily had suggested coming here. I'd told the other guys that I'd be getting to the concert before it started, but after they set up the security perimeter. We weren't primary security, just backup to the LPPD. The police often called us to help out for major events like this because of our long history with the community. Between the fun runs and other events, Padre had done a good job of keeping a good relationship with the police. The bribes helped, too.

Lisa walked past us to get to the kitchen and stopped to say hi. "I can't believe how beautiful you are, Lily," she said. "You've become a proper young woman."

We didn't come to La Passerelli very often, but when we

did, Lisa treated us right. Her husband had died of cancer and she'd raised two boys on her own while running the restaurant. She'd become friends with Padre, and then we started having Lily's birthday parties here.

We were supposed to be meeting Bailey's sister, but she was parking the car or something. The last thing I needed right now was some babbling blond older sister telling stories about pilates class or whatever chicks were into these days.

Honestly, the only woman I found myself wanting to talk to these days was Paige, but I hadn't seen her since I'd talked to Sofia. In fact, I thought it must be my imagination when I heard her voice. "Ryder?"

"Paige?"

"What are you doing here?" we both asked at the same time.

"You guys know each other?" Bailey asked.

"Oh my God. Your sister is that waitress at Tiny's." Lily looked shocked.

We were all shocked. Somehow, Paige's sister and my sister had managed to meet and become friends!

"What a small world," Paige said as she sat down next to her sister."

As soon as I saw them side by side I saw the resemblance. Bailey looked exactly like what I imagined Paige did at sixteen.

What a weird fucking coincidence. If I believed in fate, that's what I would say this was. Here I'd wanted to ask Paige to dinner and the next thing I know she walks into the restaurant I'm in so we can have dinner together!

The girls were chattering about the concert and Gerard Way's baby.

Paige tried to smooth down her wet hair and said, "If I'd known it was you I'd have dressed a little better. Honestly, I thought you were going to be some twenty-year-old kid and we'd be having Chipotle."

I had to laugh. "You look fine. Beautiful, actually. And if I'm being honest, I was expecting some ditzy bimbo."

"Oh, hey. The night is young." She laughed and I felt it all the way down to my soul. Suddenly I wanted to become Jimmy Fallon and make her laugh again.

"I wish," I said, picking up the menu. "I have to...work. My...friends and I are helping out with security for the concert. I actually should be there now but wanted to meet who Lily was going to the concert with."

"Yeah, me too. You never can be too careful these days." She was looking at me and I sensed a double meaning in her tone.

"No. It's important to have protection."

"Well, there are times when protection is overrated."

"Ew. Are you guys doing that again?" Lily wrinkled her nose and turned to Bailey. "The day we met your sister they were doing this gross flirting thing there, too."

"Oh, really?" Bailey grinned at Paige as if she'd discovered a huge secret. "Is that so?"

Fortunately, we were interrupted by the waitress who'd come to take our order.

I barely ate my lasagna. Lisa's food was as good as usual, but I was in a complete daze from running into Paige like this. It takes a lot to rattle me, but this did it.

When the girls got up to use the restroom after dinner, I finally had a chance to talk to Paige alone.

"I've been wanting to run into you again."

"You have?" She was just finishing the glass of red wine she'd had with dinner.

"Yes. There was..." The words caught in my throat, but I remembered Sofia's advice. "There was something I wanted to ask you."

"Oh? What?"

"I wanted to see if you'd like to get dinner sometime?" I was actually starting to sweat! This was ridiculous.

"You mean like we're having now?" She smiled and my heart melted. Paige was what my mother used to call "a heart-breaker."

I laughed. "Well. Yes. Like now. But more of a..."

"More of a date?" She was looking at me with those blue eyes and I almost forgot where we were.

"Yes. A date. I wanted to know if you would go out on a date with me." I felt like the biggest idiot on the planet. This was so awkward!

When she grinned, it showed deep dimples at the corners of those luscious lips.

"A date, huh? Well, I don't know. You might need to ask my dad."

"Your dad?" It was then that I realized she was teasing me. "Oh. Yeah. Well, I promise to have you home by midnight. You think that'll fly?"

"Who's going to fly?" Lily asked as she and Bailey came back from the bathroom. "I love airplanes."

PAIGE

"Thank you for dinner, Ryder. I really appreciate it." The whole meal seemed to have flown by.

"Yes. It was so good! Thank you!" Bailey added.

Thankfully, the rain let up so we wouldn't get drenched walking back to our cars. Since Ryder was going to the concert anyway, he agreed to give the girls a ride there and then bring them back to my place after. Bailey had begged for Lily to spend the night and even though I really didn't have any space other than my couch, I agreed. I remembered what it was like to be sixteen.

"I'm this way," I said to Ryder, as we stood outside the front of the restaurant.

Ryder handed his car keys to Lily. "You girls go wait in the car. I'll be right there."

"Oooooohhhhhhhh," they called as they giggled and walked away.

"They're funny," I said.

"Quite a pair, that's for sure." He stood there looking down at me. "I wanted a moment alone with you."

"Yeah," was all I could manage to say.

He took both of his hands, cupped my face, and kissed me. "I'll see you later. After the concert. Okay?"

"Okay." My head was spinning. What was happening to me?

Ryder then took off running in the direction the girls had gone. Within a minute, I was standing there alone.

"He's quite a catch." I swung around and Lisa was standing there smiling.

"Yeah." That seemed to be all I could say. It sure wasn't like me to be this tongue tied.

I was on cloud nine the whole way home. Usually it depressed the hell out of me to have to go from the beach back to North La Playa. But while I wished I could afford to live in a better neighborhood, this was giving me the life experience I needed to relate to the people in the very community I wanted to help.

I'd grown up with all the resources I needed. I didn't know what it was like to not be able to afford food. To have to use a calculator when I went through the grocery store so I wouldn't be embarrassed at having to put stuff back. I had access to health care and was able to see a doctor when I needed it.

The people I'd worked with at the free clinic in Terrance knew the struggle. And even now, while I paid my bills with tips earned as a waitress, I knew that I still had it better than most. If I got into real trouble, all I'd need to do is call my parents. A lot of folks around here didn't have that luxury.

But tonight, the city looked beautiful. The rain had made everything glisten and sparkle, and the air was heavy with moisture. The music on my car radio provided a soundtrack that made me feel like I was in some kind of movie. A movie where this was the scene when the woman realized she was falling in love.

Love? Hardly. I was being a bit dramatic, probably from the little bit of wine I'd had with dinner and the whole ambiance of the evening. It was far too soon for it to be love. Lust? Yes. Like? Definitely. Was there potential? Who knew?

But he'd sought me out to ask me to dinner. On a date.

My inner thighs tingled at the thought of that. Dates meant kissing. Kissing meant hands exploring. I wanted his hands to touch me everywhere.

Yeah, my mind and body were made up. Love or no love, I definitely wanted to have sex with Ryder. The only question would be when. Would it be tonight?

I kept my eye on the clock as I dried my hair. I'd taken a nice warm shower, shaved, and used my loofah glove. I'd put on scented lotion—not for Ryder, I told myself. For me. Because I am a woman and I enjoy feeling soft and smelling good.

If Ryder happened to benefit from it...that was fine.

I even had a rare glass of wine from a bottle I'd brought with me from my parents' wine cellar. Well, "glass" of wine wasn't exactly the right term. More like a "plastic cup" of wine. My mom would shit if she saw me drinking a $100 bottle of red wine out of a plastic Wonder Woman cup I'd gotten with a combo meal at the drive thru.

"Well, she's not here, is she?" I said to no one as I set the bottle on the kitchen counter. The place was kind of a mess, but hey. I lived alone and could do what I wanted.

The concert would be in full swing by now, so I decided to climb in bed and think about work. They should be here in about three hours, which would give me plenty of time to brainstorm ideas. There had to be some way for me to have a hands-on role in this community.

I must have sent out fifty applications in the LA area. I didn't have enough experience for most of them, or the right educational background. My cover letters were strong, but I couldn't help but wonder if they all just saw me as some rich white girl trying to have an adventure instead of a person with a passion for helping girls and women get the care they needed.

I never really knew where my passion had come from. It was just always there.

Frustrated, I threw off the covers and got out of bed. "There has to be a way." Suddenly, I heard the musical horn of the food truck that showed up about this time every Saturday night. "Andy's Asada" came by and the smells of freshly-made carne asada came wafting through my window. I'd never gotten any, but I appeared to be the only one in the neighborhood who hadn't. Within minutes each week, there was a line going around the building.

"Maybe I ought to start a food truck," I thought wryly.

Then it hit me. Maybe I really should!

RYDER

The traffic heading up Pacific Coast Highway to the convention center was a disaster. Bumper-to-bumper. The concert had sold out within minutes of the tickets going on sale, and from the line of cars, it looked like every one of the twelve thousand people had taken separate cars.

I'd be there already if it was just me on my bike. But I had a couple of very excited girls in the backseat.

"Okay, after the concert, let's meet at that Starbucks on the corner." I pointed to a Starbucks that was about four blocks away from the convention center. This way we could meet and minimize the traffic leaving the parking lot.

Since I was going to be at the concert, I'd know when it got out and would wrap things up and head over there.

"Sounds good," Lily said. "Can you let us out here? I want to check out the prices of the merch before we get inside." She was pointing to some kid with green hair selling T-shirts off the side of the road out of the back of his car.

"Sure." I pulled over and they got out. "Be careful, okay?"

Lily grinned and said, "Thanks, *Dad*. We will."

As I watched them walk over to green hair, I marveled at

how grown up she looked. And yet, she was still a girl in a lot of respects.

Shaking my head, I pulled back out into traffic. Two pretty sixteen-year-old girls alone at a concert? What could go wrong?

"'Bout time you got here." Padre was standing next to a barricade, channeling hundreds of young people into the convention center. "The rest of the guys have been here for almost two hours."

"Sorry, Padre. I had something personal come up. Did you get my text?"

"Moves said somethin' about it. You know I don't check damn texts."

It was true. Padre was really old school in a lot of ways. "What's going on here?"

"So far there's been no sign of trouble. Swole is at the north entrance with Dog, and Vlad and Moves are right across from the east entrance. Chalupa and Trainer are in the west parking lot with a clear view of that entrance. Yoda and the prospects are getting everyone coffee, and Pin is inside, watching the security cameras. You and me, we'll stake out here at the south entrance."

"Cool. Any word on whether Las Balas are planning on showing up?"

"No, but that doesn't mean they won't. They don't exactly forward us their itinerary."

I wasn't expecting them either, since this was a straightforward security gig. But with those guys you never knew. They just liked to start trouble for the hell of it sometimes.

Just then, about half a dozen LPPD bikes rolled up and parked far away from ours. Walking toward the entrance we were guarding, they completely ignored us, which was not surprising. Even though the top brass was okay with us working these events, the rank and file officers didn't appreciate our presence at all.

They went inside and we re-secured the rope that was blocking the gate.

I looked at my phone and the concert would be starting in about fifteen minutes. I found myself wondering if Lily and Bailey had found their seats okay, but before I could text to make sure, I was distracted by a loud boom out over the water.

"What the hell was that?" I asked Padre. It didn't sound like fireworks. Before he could answer, our walkie-talkies started blowing up.

"What the fuck was that?" Chalupa asked.

"Was that a goddamn bomb?"

"Everybody stay at your post!" Padre said. "It could be a diversion. It's not here on the property so let the LPPD handle it."

We were all aware of the incident last year that ended in an active shooter killing a dozen people at a concert just like this one. The cops might not be too happy that we were here, but we didn't give a fuck. Our presence was a major deterrent to shit like that happening.

For the next ten minutes or so, Padre and I just watched as cop cars and fire engines and paramedics raced down the street in the direction of the explosion.

Trainer rode up just then and parked his bike near where mine was.

"Did you hear?"

"That explosion? Yeah." The sound of sirens wailing in that direction was unmistakable.

"No. Not that. Hawk got some intel that the explosion

was at the Las Balas compound. Looks like somebody blew up their warehouse."

I shot a glance in Padre's direction. "Do we know anything about that?"

"No, man. Must be Viper's guys or somethin'."

"Well, they are sure the hell gonna think it's us."

"Look, we are on a job. We don't have time to be worrying about Las Balas or who may or may not have blown up their shit." I zipped up my jacket and headed toward the convention center entrance. "Trainer, you stay here with Padre. I'm going to go inside and see what Pin is seeing."

I just hoped that whatever was going on with Las Balas, they'd leave Outlaw Souls out of it.

The tension in the security room was as thick as the clam chowder at Tiny's. They'd heard the explosion, too, and had stepped up surveillance inside the arena where the concert was going on. At the moment, Billie Eilish was still on stage as the opening act, but MCR was going on in about twenty minutes.

"What's the latest?" I asked Pin.

"So far everything is going as planned. No one doing anything suspicious that we can tell."

Given the fact that the small room was jammed with cops, venue security, and us, it looked like they were expecting a problem.

"What was the explosion, do we know yet?" Pin asked.

I lowered my voice so that only he could hear. "Hawk said that someone blew up the Las Balas compound."

"Shit. They're gonna think it was us."

"I know. So that's why I came in here. You need to keep a close eye out for any of their guys, because they are gonna be looking for some serious revenge. The cops won't necessarily think of that and we don't want to call attention to it, so let's just all be on the lookout."

"You got it, boss."

I wondered if Scorpion knew where Lily and Bailey were sitting. Maybe I ought to just go check and make sure they were okay.

When it was decked out for a concert, the convention center could seat about 12,000 people. Bailey had gotten them floor seats (further evidence that she came from money) and they were about a third of the way back from the stage. The security room was underground in a maze of tunnels that led to various parts of the venue. It was how celebrities and other notables got in and out without being seen.

I was walking down a long, brightly lit hallway with cement walls and shiny white tiles, headed to the entrance that would get me closest to the stage when a door opened and four guys came out, escorted by three security people. I immediately recognized the middle one as Gerard Way, the lead singer of My Chemical Romance. His posters had been plastered all over Lily's bedroom for years. She was going to shit when I told her I met him.

"Hey," I said.

"Hey," he said as we all started walking in the same direction. His voice sounded a lot higher than I thought it would.

"Good luck tonight, guys. It's a full house out there," I said. It seemed lame, but I didn't know what else to say.

"Thanks. I love it when people come out to see us." He smiled and seemed like a really down-to-earth person.

"What does your jacket say?" asked one of the other guys.

I wasn't up on my MCR knowledge and I didn't honestly know who he was.

"Outlaw Souls." Our logo was a pair of angel wings and over it was a pair of handcuffs where the halo would have been.

"You're an MC?"

"Yeah." We were approaching the door to the stage. I was going to keep going a bit to get to the audience level.

"We're in MCR," said another guy.

"Practically the same thing," said the fourth and they all laughed.

"Well, thanks for watching out for us. We appreciate it," Gerard said.

"It's the least I could do. My sister is convinced you're going to marry her someday." Never mind the fact that Gerard was in his forties and already married and had a kid.

"Aw. That's sweet." He then took the hair tie out of his hair and gave it to me. "Give this to her. I'd sign it, but... you can't really sign a hair tie and that's all I have." It was black leather and said MCR.

Lily was definitely going to freak out. "This will mean a lot to her, thanks." I stuffed the hair tie in my jacket.

The door to the stage opened and we could hear Billie thanking the audience. The lights would come up and it would be my opportunity to check on Lily and Bailey without them knowing I was there.

PAIGE

I couldn't help it, but I kept watching the clock. The romantic mood of earlier had dissipated and I just felt edgy and anxious. Was it all the stuff with Ryder? Was my gut instinct telling me to slow down with him? Maybe wait before jumping into bed?

I honestly couldn't tell. It was about 9 pm and I imagined the main performance would be starting about now. My apartment felt really stuffy and I wanted to get out of here. But I really didn't have anywhere to go. The girls would be home by midnight and I didn't want to spend the money on a movie or anything. I didn't really have any friends and my parents lived too far away. And they thought I was at the concert with Bailey.

I'd spent about an hour fleshing out a business idea that I wanted to run by my dad, but it would have to wait.

There was nothing on TV either. Why the hell did we pay for 400 TV channels when there was never anything on other than Guy Fieri, news, sports, or movies from 2002?

Turning it off, I grabbed my car keys. Maybe I'd head out to Southgate Martinez and pick up some snacks for the girls to have tonight when they got home. If their concert experience was anything like mine was, they'd definitely have the munchies when they got back.

———

Since Southgate was at the intersection with Tiny's on one corner, the Blue Dog Saloon on another, and the gas station on the third corner, I had a good view of everything going on. Tiny's was closed, as a lot of our customers were senior citizens and it wasn't cost-effective to stay open past 8:00 pm. The Blue Dog was pretty empty too, probably because the Outlaw Souls were doing security for the concert. It was just a quiet Saturday night in the 'hood.

As I was walking inside, my phone buzzed. The caller ID said it was my mom, but I knew I couldn't answer the phone because she thought I was at the concert. I sent her to voicemail and then walked in the store.

All of the signage in the entire store was in Spanish. I'd taken it in high school, but really didn't know it very well. If I were going to stay in this community, I should probably learn it, I figured.

Grabbing a cart, I made my way through the bakery, successfully avoiding the delicious-looking pan dulce and other pastries. What would they like? Maybe I'd get something sweet and something savory. I swung back and picked up two bright pink sweet breads, a package of cinnamon rolls for breakfast, and headed over to the tortilleria to grab the ingredients for soft tacos.

"Hola. Como estas?" I turned around and this guy was standing way too close to me. He smelled like beer and weed, and his greasy hair was slicked back in an attempt to look cool. But I could see flecks of dandruff.

He was way too close, so I took a step back and gave him that social nod thing and kept walking.

"No habla espanol? You don't speak Spanish?" He was following me, holding a thirty-two ounce bottle of beer.

I really didn't want to talk to him so I just ignored him and kept walking. He didn't give up and kept following me.

"What's the matter, blondie? You think you're too good to talk to a cholo?"

"Look. I'm just trying to do some shopping here. Why don't you go do the same?"

"You bitches are all the same." He shook his head and muttered something in Spanish as he walked toward the register.

My tension level went down and I went to go grab some freshly-made guacamole to go with the tacos. *See? It's all about projecting an air of confidence.* I could handle myself in this neighborhood just fine.

Fifteen minutes later, my cart was loaded up with snacks and drinks and stuff to make a late dinner when the girls got home. It cost me $30 that hadn't been in my tight budget, but that was okay. I wanted Bailey and Lily to have a good time.

The hatchback to the Honda was open and I was quickly putting the bags in when that same guy from inside the store stepped out from behind the van that was parked next to me. He was holding the beer, but it was almost empty.

"You ready to party, blondie?"

My stomach lurched in fear. The parking lot was basically empty and there wasn't anyone around to help me.

"Leave me alone." I quickly reached up to grab the hatch-back so I could get the hell out of there.

"What's the matter, blondie? You don't like Mexican

food?" He laughed at his own joke and held up the beer bottle. "I saved you a drink."

My hands were shaking as I grabbed my keys. I'd seen a video where you could punch someone in the eyes with keys that were wedged between your fingers. I just wanted to get in my car and leave, honestly.

My free hand reached out to grab the car door and he slammed me up against the car, facing away from him.

His hot breath was on my ear and I could feel him pressing against my back, pinning me against the car. "You're being rude, blondie. Don't be a bitch."

My mouth went dry with fear. "Please let me go." I didn't like how scared I sounded.

He grabbed me by the waist and pumped his pelvis into my rear end a few times, like a dog dry humping a pant leg. He took one hand and grabbed my throat so hard I thought I was going to choke.

"Trust me, blondie. You'd be begging me not to let you go. But I ain't playing like that." He let me go, staggered back a few feet, laughing and looking at me.

My whole body was shaking as I pulled open the car door and climbed inside, locking it behind me. I could see him still standing there, just laughing and drinking beer.

"It's your loss, blondie. You go and tell all your rich bitch friends that you had some prime Mexican meat and you threw it away." He then went back into the shadows as I started my car.

I was hyperventilating and crying by the time I pulled out onto Berry Avenue. I didn't want to pull over. I just wanted to get home.

RYDER

I opened the door to the floor section of the convention center just as MCR were coming onstage. Because of that, the whole place was sheer madness. Everyone was standing and screaming and holding up phones. The room was dark, except for laser lights flashing. The sights and sounds were intense.

There was no way I'd be able to find Lily and Bailey in this chaos. They did have assigned seats, but every single person in the venue was out of their seat. It was a security nightmare.

I retreated back into the relative quiet of the hallway. I figured I'd try and contact them another way, so I pulled out my phone.

Having fun? Text me and show me how great your view is!

Unfortunately, the reception here was terrible and there was a red check next to the message that told me it hadn't gone through. I'd have to go outside and retry it, but for now I was just going to have to trust that Lily and Bailey were fine, that they'd made it here okay.

Time to get back out and find Padre to see what was going on. Even though everything seemed to be going smoothly, I couldn't shake the feeling that something was going to happen. I didn't know what, and I didn't know with whom. But my spidey sense was up.

The air smelled like burning rubber when I stepped outside the doors of the convention center. "What's up?" I asked Swole as I passed her checkpoint.

"That fire is still burning by the waterfront and half of the LPPD are out there. It's a good thing we're here, because as of the moment, there's not enough cops if something did go wrong."

"That's the thing that concerns me, Swole. I can't help but wonder if the explosion and fire were some kind of diversion for something else that's about to happen."

She nodded in agreement. "Exactly."

I patted her arm and mentally marveled again at her rock hard biceps. "You keep an eye out. I'm gonna go talk to Padre."

"Sounds good."

Since the concert was in full swing, there weren't very many people outside the venue. I could hear thumping and applause coming from inside, and sirens coming from the waterfront fire.

As I approached him, Padre's back was to me and he appeared to be alone. Where the hell was Trainer? Someone was supposed to be with Padre at all times.

I was about to ask, but I heard his voice speaking softly and he was on the phone.

"Yes, it's under control. I told you it would be. You just handle things on your end and let me worry about mine."

I stepped on a soda bottle and it made a crunching sound, which alerted Padre to my presence. He whipped around and then said, "I'll bring some milk on the way home." Ending the call, he said, "What did you find, Ryder?"

Where was Trainer? Was Padre really on the phone with his wife, or was he pretending? What was under control? The lack-of-milk situation didn't seem to warrant hushed tones.

"What do you mean?" I asked.

"Inside. With Pin. Is everything okay there?"

"Oh, yeah. Fine." I looked around. "Where's Trainer?"

"He had to go take a leak."

I shook my head. So much for keeping an eye on Padre.

Just then, Trainer walked up. "There you are!" he said to Padre. "Where the fuck did you go?"

"I was using the can. You got a problem with that?" Padre said.

The whole scene was confusing me. Trainer was looking for Padre, but Padre said Trainer went to the bathroom. Who was looking for who?

Suddenly, all of our walkie talkies lit up at the same time.

"Something is happening. Get in here NOW!" Swole said. *"I heard three pops, like gunshots, and everyone is screaming and running!"* That sounded like Chalupa but I couldn't be sure.

Sure enough, people were starting to pour out of the exits, running and screaming. My heart froze and I instantly sprung to action. Lily. I needed to find Lily.

I didn't even wait for Padre. I just started running toward the first door I could get to.

If the outside of the convention center was chaos, the inside was ten times worse. All of the lights were up and a voice was speaking over the sound system. "Please exit the building in an orderly manner. Do not panic or run. Proceed to the nearest exit."

No one was listening. I was pushing my way through the crowd, but there were so many people trying to get by me that I was being pushed backward anyway.

Finally, I stood flat against the wall and crept forward that way.

"Was it a shooter?" Trainer asked on the walkie talkie. "Has anyone been shot?"

"I don't know yet. The LPPD are securing the scene. I am inside and don't see any injuries except for some people who fell while running. There are gonna be some broken bones and stuff." That was Hawk.

I had no idea how I was going to find Lily in this mess. Part of me wanted to just take off and go to the meeting point, but I also knew I couldn't leave until we knew what was going on.

"Please exit the building in an orderly manner. Do not panic or run. Proceed to the nearest exit."

People were panicking and running. Finally, I made it to the internal door of the arena and pushed my way through the throng of people coming up the stairs to get out the door. I was on a higher level and could see the floor seats below me. People were scrambling to get out, but I saw no evidence of anyone who'd been shot or was bleeding. Swole was down there guiding people out, and I could see several of the other guys doing the same thing.

Still no sign of Lily.

"Help me!" A young woman was pinned against a barrier. "I'm stuck."

"I'm on my way," I shouted, grabbing people by their jackets and shirts and literally throwing them to the side. As I got close, I saw that the woman had a child with her that she was shielding from getting trampled. They were both pressed tightly up against a barricade and the crowd was pressing them into it. The little girl was crying.

"Here, let me have your hand," I said to the girl. She appeared to be about eight years old or so and had black braids all around her head. I pulled her close enough to grab her waist and then lifted her up over the crowd. "Put your legs on my shoulders and I'll give you a piggyback ride out of here, okay?"

Her mom was cradling her left arm with her right and I asked, "Are you hurt?"

She nodded. "Yeah, I think my arm is broken."

"Okay, let's get you out of here."

"My friend. My friend is still missing," she said, looking around frantically.

"That's okay. We need to get you out of here and to see a doctor. MOVE ASIDE," I said in my most commanding voice. "We need to get through."

One of the main advantages of being six feet tall and covered with tattoos is that people pretty much do what you say. They took one look at me with the little girl on my shoulders and her injured mom and made room for us.

Just outside the entrance to the venue, there were police cars set up in a perimeter. We walked up to one of the officers and I said, "This lady is hurt and needs medical attention." He took the girl from me, nodded, and then escorted them to a nearby ambulance.

I was relieved that there had been no more reports of gunshots, or what sounded like them. But the scene was still crazy and no one had any idea what had happened.

For a moment, I stood there torn. I wanted to rush off to the Starbucks where Lily and Bailey and I were to meet up. But there was no way I could leave now, so I headed back inside to see who else needed my help. Before I did, though, I sent Lily another text.

Are you guys okay? Please text back.

Unfortunately, my first text hadn't gone through, and this one came back "undelivered" too.

Where are you, Lily?

PAIGE

I couldn't catch my breath. I'd managed to drive the short distance home from Southgate, but I was having a full-blown panic attack in the car. I couldn't even get out and go into my apartment. I was just sitting there, frozen in fear, with my hands covering my face as I tried to regulate my breathing. I couldn't stop feeling his hands on me.

Knock knock knock. Someone rapped on the car window and I almost jumped out of my skin. I was surprised I didn't scream.

"Hey, are you okay?" It was the woman who lived on the first floor, directly under my apartment.

I couldn't move and so I just shook my head no. I was definitely not okay.

"Hey. Unlock the door. Let me help." She was standing right outside my window, crouching down. "It's okay. I can help you."

My hand felt around on the car door for the lock and I pressed the button. As soon as she heard the click she opened the car door and kneeled down, facing me.

"What happened? Are you hurt?"

I shook my head no, and she touched my arm. "Come on. Let's get you inside. You can come to my place for a few minutes."

Her words and her touch woke me out of the shock I was in. I unbuckled my seat belt and grabbed my bag and purse. "Thank you, I'm sorry. I just..."

She put her arm around me protectively and we walked into the building together. My knees were weak and my legs were wobbly, and I was very happy when she locked the door behind us at her place.

She took my bags and set them on a small metal card table in the living room. "Your name is Paige, right?"

I nodded. "Yes. I live right above you."

"I know! My name is Maria."

I'd seen her a bunch of times coming and going, but we'd never actually talked.

"Come sit down. I'll make you some tea."

As I crossed over to the plaid couch, I got a look at her place. It was the same layout as my apartment, but of course it looked different with her furniture in it.

She had a television going with a Spanish channel on it, and on the bookshelf next to the TV were pictures of Maria with a young boy I'd seen with her before and had assumed was her son.

My apartment hardly had any furniture and felt bare, but hers felt homey and lived in. "How long have you lived at Banner Manor?" I asked.

"Oh, about five years. I came right after Mario was born." She nodded to some photos on the fridge. "He is with his Tia this weekend. His dad may have run off on me, but his family has been good to us."

My heart rate was starting to calm down as she handed me the tea. "Thank you."

"So what happened to you?" she asked, sitting down next to me on the couch.

"I was...attacked in the Southgate parking lot."

Her eyes flew open wide. "Ay dios mio! Are you all right?"

"Yeah, he just scared me. That's all."

"You should call the cops. Or see a doctor?"

I didn't need a doctor, but I did wonder if I could call the police. Then again, it had been about half an hour and I wasn't even sure I would be able to recognize the guy. On the other hand, there might be cameras in the parking lot of Southgate.

"I don't know. Maybe..."

Just as I took my first sip of tea, some breaking news interrupted the show that was on the TV. I didn't understand what they were saying, but there was a reporter standing outside the La Playa Convention Center. There were a ton of cops and fire trucks and ambulances there.

"Oh my God." My heart started pounding again. "My sister is there."

Maria looked at the TV and grabbed the remote to turn up the volume.

"What are they saying?" I asked. It appeared to be sheer chaos.

"They are saying that there was a shooting at the concert. They don't know how many casualties there were but that the shooter has not been captured."

I started shaking uncontrollably. "I have to go. I have to get to my sister."

"You are in no condition to drive, Paige."

I had my phone out and my hands were shaking as I tried to text Bailey. The message didn't go through, so I tried to call and it went straight to voicemail.

I was full on panicking now, so I tried to call Ryder. Same thing. It went straight to voicemail.

"I'm sorry, Maria. I have to go." I stood up and was patting my pants to find my keys. "Where are my keys?!"

"Paige. Look. If you must go, let me drive you. You really are too upset to drive. You were upset when you got here."

She was right. "Okay, thank you. But please, let's hurry."

What a terrible night. I'd insisted on listening to news radio on the way downtown. Maria had a Toyota truck and I was in the passenger seat, flipping from station to station trying to get news on the shooting. Every station had a different story.

One station was saying that it was a gang-related shootout. Another was saying it was a lone shooter. A third station said that there was no evidence of a shooter at all, that no one had been reported at local hospitals with gunshot wounds and it was likely all a hoax.

A hoax? Who would do such a terrible thing? I kept trying to contact Bailey and Ryder. If I'd had Lily's number, I'd have called her too.

The freeway was jammed because the exit to the convention center was closed off. Not surprising, really.

"Maybe if we take the next exit and circle back we can get close."

We got off the freeway and were going down Pacific Drive and I could see some building burning in the distance. The sky was filled with helicopters—probably both news and police. The air smelled like burning rubber.

The inside of the truck lit up from an incoming call. It was my mother. As much as I didn't want to talk to her, I knew she'd probably heard the news and was worried. I had to take the call.

"Hi Mom."

"Oh my God, Paige. I'm so glad you both are all right. What's going on? Did you and Bailey see anything?"

"Hey. Yeah. There's something I need to tell you..."

RYDER

We were all standing outside in the parking lot. We'd helped get everyone out of the convention center and then the LPPD took over, working with venue security. Our night here was over.

"Did they ever catch the shooter?" Chalupa asked.

"There's not even evidence that there WAS a shooter. Witnesses said they heard three loud pops that sounded like gunfire and then everyone started screaming and running." Hawk lit up a cigarette.

"So no victims with gunshot wounds?" Trainer asked.

Hawk shook his head. "I can't say for sure, but it doesn't seem like it."

I was listening, but I wasn't. I needed to get to the Starbucks to meet up with Lily. "Look, guys. I need to take off. I'm supposed to meet my sister at that Starbucks."

"Oh my God, that's right. Your sister was here!" Swole said. "Have you seen her?"

"No. And her phone is going straight to voicemail." I'd tried so many times that I killed my own battery.

"No worries, Ryder. See you back at the shop. Take care of Lily," Chalupa said.

Padre was strangely silent and for a minute I remembered the conversation I'd overheard. But I didn't have time to worry about that. I needed to find my sister.

Not for the first time tonight, I was regretting that I had the car instead of my bike. If I'd had the bike, I would have already been parked and inside Starbucks. But, because of everything that had gone down tonight and the streets being blocked off around the convention center, it took me half an hour to find a spot four blocks away.

The clock in the car said it was 11:30 pm. I hoped the Starbucks would still be open and that the girls knew to stay safely inside until I got there.

Judging from the number of people milling around outside, it was a good chance that the place was still open. Hopefully, I could find the girls, get back to the car, and be at Paige's place within the hour.

Paige... I wondered if she had heard the news. If so, she must have been so worried. There were tons of helicopters still overhead and news vans everywhere. Plus, given the number of rumors flying around, who knew what she thought happened?

It was a terrible time for my phone to be dead, for sure.

As I approached the Starbucks, I had my eyes out for Bailey. She was tall and blond like Paige and would be easier to spot than my dark-haired sister.

"Bailey!" I said, as I walked up to a blonde waiting outside the front door. But when she turned around, I saw that it wasn't her. "Sorry."

"No worries. Everyone's looking for someone tonight."

I scanned the crowd outside and didn't see them so I figured I'd go inside. They were probably sitting there having a Frappuccino and tweeting about their adventure.

The place was packed, but I didn't see Lily or Bailey anywhere. I was getting worried and I went back up to Not Bailey and tapped her on the shoulder. "Excuse me. Can you do me a favor?"

She smiled. "Sure. What?"

"Can you go into the ladies' room and see if my sister and her friend are in there?"

"Oh, sure."

I followed her over to the small hallway where the bathrooms were. Most Starbucks have gender-neutral bathrooms these days, but this one had a throwback ladies' room, too.

"What are their names?" she asked.

"Lily. Lily and Bailey."

"Pretty names. Okay, hang on, I'll be right back."

Instinctively I checked my phone before I remembered that it was dead. One minute later she came out and shook her head. "Unless your sister is an old Asian woman, she's not in there."

Dammit. Where could they be? "Okay, thank you for checking."

I decided to charge my phone. Maybe they'd sent a text message about where they would be. I plugged in a nearby outlet and looked around at the people hugging and crying, reuniting with loved ones. There were still so many questions about what happened tonight. What was the explosion at the waterfront? Was it the Las Balas compound? If so, who did it? Was it related to the event at the concert? Was there really a shooter, and if so, where did he or she go? Was anyone actually shot? What was the motive?

Despite all of that, there was only one question I cared about getting the answer to. Where was Lily?

PAIGE

I hated to have to tell my mom that we'd lied to her, but there was no way around it. "Mom, I didn't go to the concert with Bailey."

"What? Yes you did. You picked her up this afternoon."

"I know. But Bailey went with a friend."

"A friend? What friend? Was it a boy?" My poor mom sounded confused.

"No, it was a girl. Her name is Lily. I met her and we had dinner together." It seemed like a month ago that we'd gone to La Passarelli.

"Why would your sister lie about going to a concert with a girlfriend? Is she a lesbian?"

"God, Mom!" I swear, that woman was stuck in 1978. "She didn't want you to know because Lily lives in La Playa and she thought you would be judgy about it."

There was silence on the other end of the phone and I could hear my dad in the background. "Is everything all right? Are the girls okay?" he asked.

"So you're telling me that you dropped Bailey off at the La

Playa Convention Center with some girl you just met tonight and now you don't know where she is?" my mom continued.

I decided to leave out the part about the guy from the motorcycle gang that dropped them off instead of me and just said, "Pretty much, yes."

"That's it. We're coming down."

"Mom, I'm not even home. I'm looking for Bailey."

"This is not up for discussion, Paige. Bailey is still my child and your father and I are coming down."

I knew the tone of her voice meant she was serious and there was nothing I could say that would dissuade her. "Do you still have a key?" They'd insisted on having a spare key to my place "in case of emergency." Looked like they were right to do it. This was definitely an emergency.

"Yes. We'll be there within the hour."

"Okay. I'm almost to the convention center now. I'll let you know what I find out."

"Good." She sounded pissed.

"Oh, and Mom?"

"Yes?"

"I'm sorry we lied."

"I am too." The line disconnected and I felt like I was ten years old again and had broken a piece of her favorite china.

Except this was her daughter, and if something serious happened to Bailey, they would never forgive me. I'd never be able to forgive myself, either.

It wasn't too surprising that the entire section of the city where the convention center was was blocked off. Maria pulled her truck up to one of the barriers and I rolled down my window to talk to one of the police officers.

"Excuse me. Where did the people go who were attending the concert?"

"Some of them have been taken to La Playa Memorial. Some are still inside being interviewed by police. But most of the crowd dispersed two hours ago. Are you looking for someone?"

"Yes. My sister and her friend."

"My recommendation would be to start with the hospital and then go from there."

"Were there any... fatalities?" I hated to ask the question.

"I'm afraid I can't say."

You can't say, or you won't?

"What about the Outlaw Souls? They were here helping with security. Where are they?"

"Oh, we sent them home about an hour ago. We're inside reviewing security footage and once the crowd was gone we didn't need crowd control."

Dammit. I couldn't find Ryder or Lily or Bailey.

"Okay, thanks." I turned to Maria. "It looks like it's gonna be a long night for me. If you want to drop me off somewhere, I can take an Uber to the hospital."

"No way. I'll take you there now."

"Thanks. I really appreciate it. You're going way far out of your way for someone you just met." As we were pulling out of the parking lot, I remembered there was a Starbucks down the block. "Can I get you a coffee or something to say thank you?"

"Honestly, that sounds really good about now."

The news was still talking about what had happened, but there was no real information coming out. My plan was to get some coffee, get to the hospital, and see if the girls were there. I couldn't decide whether I wanted them to be there or not.

I was glad the Starbucks was still open. The hours posted said they closed at 11:00 but there were still a ton of people inside. It had been a very traumatic experience for a lot of people and when that happened, people tended to want to come together.

Maria had a handicapped placard that she said was from a back injury from when she was pregnant with Mario, and so we were able to park right in front. I was really worried about the girls and just wanted to run in, grab a couple of coffees, and get to the hospital. If the Starbucks had been a drive thru, we wouldn't have even gotten out of the car.

"Let's just grab our coffees and get to the hospital. I'm sure your sister is just fine," Maria said, gently touching my arm.

"I hope you're right."

"What can I get started for you tonight?" The older woman behind the register was probably the owner and was working so that her employees could go home. Given how packed the place was, she would likely be here all night.

"Just a tall Americano," I said.

"Same," Maria said.

As I stuck my debit card chip into the machine, I looked around at all the people here. So many people hugging and crying or looking worried on the phone.

Speaking of which, I pulled my phone out to see if maybe, just maybe, Bailey had written back.

My heart leapt when I saw that I had a text message. It wasn't from Bailey, but it was from Ryder.

Hey. Where are you? I've been trying to call!

I looked at my phone and somehow the ringer had been turned off.

OMG I'm sorry. My ringer was off. Where are you? Have you heard from the girls? What happened tonight?

I haven't heard from the girls, and I'm still not really sure what happened at the event. I'm at the Starbucks where we were supposed to meet up, but they're not here.

I'm at a Starbucks too. Which one are you at?

The one on Third Street about four blocks from the convention center.

My head shot up from my phone and looked around. Ryder was here? Maria came over and handed me my coffee. "Are you ready to go?"

"Wait. The brother of my sister's friend is here!" I was looking all around.

"The who of your what?" she asked.

"My sister went to the concert with a friend. Her brother is here!" Just then, I saw his dark hair over by the restrooms. "Ryder!"

His head raised at the sound of his name and I had never been happier to see a familiar face in my life.

"Oh Ryder!" I ran across the crowded room and straight into his arms. Tears I didn't know I'd been holding back came streaming out and I pressed my face into his chest. "I am so glad you're here."

The smell of his leather jacket was very comforting and I felt safe in his arms. Between the attack in the parking lot and the girls going missing, there was a lot of pent-up emotion as I'd been trying to hold it together.

I heard someone clear their throat and realized that Maria was standing right there.

"Oh, I'm sorry!" I said, wiping my tears away. "Ryder, this is my neighbor Maria. Maria, this is..."

"The brother of the friend of your sister." She was smiling. "Nice to meet you."

"The police told me to check at La Playa Memorial and so we stopped for some coffee on our way," I said.

"I'm glad you did. I was supposed to meet the girls here after the concert but they never showed." He stood to grab his trash and said, "Let's go to the hospital together."

I looked at Maria, who said, "No worries. I'll go home and keep your parents company."

"Maria, you've done so much. You should just go home and rest."

She smiled and said, "What are new amigas for?" Holding up her coffee, she said, "Besides. I just had coffee. I can go talk their ears off until you get home."

We exchanged phone numbers so that I could keep her updated and then we hugged before she left. She leaned in close and whispered, "That is one fine-looking man, and he's definitely into you."

I didn't know how she could tell from having met him for five minutes, but I wasn't going to question it. I had other things on my mind...

RYDER

As soon as my phone powered on, my heart sank. No calls or texts from Lily. There were several missed calls from Paige, and that's why I decided to text her. Little did I know she was standing a few feet away from me.

I had to admit, it felt pretty amazing to have her run straight into my arms. A guy could definitely get used to that.

But first we needed to get to the hospital. I honestly didn't think that Lily or Bailey would be there. There didn't appear to have been any fatalities or major injuries from tonight's chaos, according to the news. If one of them had been hurt, the other surely would have contacted us.

I didn't have a good feeling about this at all, but didn't want to freak Paige out, so I didn't say anything to her about it.

It took about twenty minutes to get from downtown La Playa to the hospital. This time of night normally doesn't have any traffic, and I was glad that the hospital parking lot wasn't too crowded.

I stole a glance at Paige as we were looking for a parking space. Despite the chaos of the evening, she looked gorgeous.

She'd changed since dinner and her hair was up in one of those messy buns that looked sexy and casual. My body started to remember our passionate kiss from earlier, but my mind stayed focused on the task at hand. Find the girls.

"I hope they're here, Ryder," she said as we pulled the car into a space next to the Emergency Room. "I can't imagine why no one has contacted us."

I reached over to squeeze her hand and said with more confidence than I felt, "Everything is going to be okay." Maybe if I said it, it would be true.

The line for the information desk wasn't long, but the woman behind the computer must have been a hundred years old. We stood there for a good fifteen minutes while she yelled "What?" and "Could you speak up?" to the people in front of us.

Finally, it was our turn. "Hi. Our sisters were at the convention center tonight and we wondered if they had been brought here."

"What?" she said. Her brown eyes were watery and her dark skin was so wrinkled it looked like a fabric bag that had been through the washer too many times.

"Our sisters. We need to know if they are here." I enunciated very clearly.

She looked at Paige. "Is this your sister?"

"No. We both have sisters and we want to know if they are here," Paige said. This would be funny if we weren't so worried.

"Oh. Okay. What's your sister's name?"

"Mine is Lily Hernandez."

The woman started to hunt and peck on the keyboard.

"And mine is Bailey Anton."

Her head shot up. "Which is it?"

"Both," we said in unison.

She gave us a blank look and then said, "Your sister has all those names?"

"No! There are two sisters!" I was looking around for her supervisor. This was ridiculous.

"Oh. Why didn't you just say so? What are their names?"

Paige shot me a look and I took a deep breath. I have never wanted to punch an old woman in my life, but this one was coming close.

"Lily Hernandez. L-I-L-Y."

"What? Can you speak up?"

It took us almost half an hour to find out that Lily and Bailey were not at the hospital. While part of me was relieved, the bigger part of me was really worried. Where the hell could they be?

"So, tell me what happened again? From the beginning?" Paige was sitting in the front seat of my car with her knees up, hugging them.

"We left La Passarelli when you saw us. We were a few blocks from the convention center and they wanted to be let out so that they could see some T-shirts and stuff this guy was selling. We were going to meet up at the Starbucks after the concert."

"And you never saw them again after that?"

"No. After the explosion by the waterfront..."

"Wait, what?"

"There was an explosion by the waterfront a few minutes before everything went down inside the convention center."

"What kind of explosion?"

I shook my head and decided not to get into it. "No one

knew. But needless to say the security team was on alert. So I went and tried to find the girls in their seats but the band was just coming on stage and it was too crazy to see anything."

Paige was frowning and had a confused expression. "Okay. So then what?"

"Then I went outside to talk to Padre and someone inside the convention center heard three pops that they thought was gunfire, and evidently everyone else did too, because people started running out of every door. I went in to try and find them, but people were getting trampled and by the time I made it to the floor, they were gone."

"And then you went to the meet up place and they weren't there either."

"Right." We just sat there in silence for a bit, each lost in our own thoughts.

"Should we go to the police?"

I shook my head. "There's no point yet. Two sixteen-year-old girls go to a concert and they don't show up at the appointed meeting place after the concert? It doesn't exactly sound fishy."

"Right, but Bailey would never just not call. It's completely out of character for her."

I wished I could say the same thing about Lily. I knew the next person I needed to talk to, and did not want Paige to be with me for it. "Look. Why don't I take you home and I'll talk to some people and see what our next move is?"

She sighed. "Normally, I'd say that I wanted to keep looking but my parents are at my apartment and I'd better get over there and do some damage control. Poor Maria is alone with them."

I started the car and pulled out of the space to head back to North La Playa. While Paige was going to be doing damage control, the rage filling my belly told me that I was about to do some serious damage myself.

PAIGE

I could see the lights still on in Maria's apartment as Ryder pulled up front. I really didn't want to go in there, partly because I wanted to stay with Ryder and partly because I didn't want to deal with my parents.

What I wanted was to be inside my apartment, eating tacos with Bailey and Lily. Tears sprang to my eyes. What would I do if something happened to her?

"Don't think about it, Paige," Ryder said. He reached out and pulled me over for a hug. "I will find the girls. I promise you that, okay?"

I looked in his face and saw fierce determination. He would find them.

He opened his car door and came around to let me out. "Let me walk you to the door."

The last thing I needed was to be questioned by my parents, so I said, "Just stay and watch me walk in from here, okay?"

"Okay."

I wrapped my arms around him, inside of his leather jacket, for a hug. He felt so good and strong that I never wanted to leave. Reluctantly, I pulled back. "Keep me posted, okay? Call me as soon as you know anything."

"I will."

I then walked the path up to Maria's apartment, dreading what waited for me inside.

"Where have you been?" My mother stood up from the couch as soon as Maria closed the door behind me. "Where's Bailey? Did she go up to your apartment?"

"Rosemary, let the girl inside before you start peppering her with questions." My dad's face was literally pale with worry.

"I just want to know, Russell. Where is your sister, Paige?"

I took a deep breath and said, "I don't know. We couldn't find her."

"You don't know? What do you mean you don't know? First you lie to us about going to the concert with your sister, and then you LOSE HER?"

"I'm sorry. I don't know what happened, honestly."

Maria was looking at me empathetically. "I'm sorry, Paige."

"Come on, Russell. Hand me my purse. We're going to the police to sort this out."

My dad stood up and was looking around for my mother's Louis Vuitton bag.

"Mom. The police aren't going to do anything. She's sixteen and is late coming home from a concert."

"Like hell they won't," she said.

"Look. Why don't we go upstairs to my apartment and let Maria get some sleep? We'll wait a little while and if we don't hear anything by morning, I'll drive us to the police station."

My mother looked at my dad, and he said, "She's making

sense, Rosemary. They won't do anything until at least the morning."

Maria went to the fridge and got the bag of food I'd bought earlier at Southgate. For a moment I remembered the attack, but I put it out of my mind as fast as possible. "Thank you so much for everything, Maria."

"Of course, amiga. Keep me posted, okay?"

I hugged her and ushered my parents out her front door. "My place is up here."

I opened the door and held it for my parents to go in first. It was strange to go inside and see everything as if I were seeing it for the first time through their eyes. When I'd left the apartment earlier this evening, I was just running out for a few minutes to get some snacks for the girls. Now, it was 2:00 am, I'd been accosted in a parking lot, Bailey had gone missing, and my parents were standing in my living room.

The apartment was really bare. Just a leather couch I'd gotten from the thrift store, along with a coffee table that I'd found by a dumpster outside of Tiny's. I was using inverted milk crates as end tables, which I thought was a very clever idea until I saw my mother staring at them.

"Are these my lamps?" she said.

"No, those are the ones I got at the Hendersons' garage sale last year and was storing in our garage."

"Ah. I thought they looked familiar."

We were all really worried about Bailey. But there was nothing any of us could do now but wait, and maybe it would get our minds off of it.

"Wait a minute. Is this my 2017 Caymus Cabernet?" my mother said, holding up the bottle I'd snagged from her wine cellar. "That you're drinking out of a...Wonder Woman cup?"

Damn. I wasn't exactly expecting company. "Oh, yeah. I've been meaning to thank you for that."

"Thank me?" She looked confused.

"Yeah. For the housewarming gift."

"I didn't give you a..."

"Anyway, come over here and sit down. You can have a glass of the wine if you'd like, Mom."

Both of my parents came to sit on the couch.

"Is that bruise on your neck? It looks like a handprint."

My hand instinctively flew up to my neck and I raced to the bathroom. Sure enough, looking back at me through the cloudy mirror was a handprint. From that asshole in the parking lot. I had a mark on my neck from where he had his disgusting hands on me.

The panic and fear that I'd been holding back came rushing out. That experience had been traumatic enough. What if Bailey and Lily were being held captive right now?

I started to hyperventilate and cry.

"Paige? Are you okay?" My dad came into the bathroom. "What's the matter, honey?" I didn't want to tell them what had happened to me, because it would just confirm their feeling that I wasn't safe living here and couldn't handle myself.

On the other hand, I was standing in my bathroom with a big purple handprint on my neck hyperventilating and crying.

I grabbed some toilet paper and blew my nose. How was I going to get out of this?

Finally I decided that it was time to stop lying to them about stuff. No more covering for Bailey. No more shielding them from the truth about me and my life. I was a grown woman and I didn't have to be worried that my mommy and daddy would be mad at me.

"Come on in here, Dad."

He followed me to where Mom was sitting. My mom looked worried but sat there quietly.

"I was attacked in the parking lot of the grocery store tonight."

"What?" My dad looked horrified. "What happened?"

I was about to tell them the story when my mom's face went pale and she said, "Oh no. Not you, too."

RYDER

I'd had enough of driving this car and really wanted to be on my bike. Now that Paige was safely home, my mind was focused on finding Lily and Bailey. I had to force the terrible thoughts from my mind about what could be happening to them. Best case scenario was that the girls had gone off to meet up with Scorpion and they were having some relatively harmless fun.

Worst case scenario was...well...worse.

As much as I wanted to drop off the car and get my bike, I needed to have a vehicle that could also fit Bailey if I found them. Lily was used to being on the back of the bike.

So, instead of going home, I went to the Blue Dog. I wanted to talk to Hawk and see what he knew about the explosion and see if he'd heard anything about the girls.

When I pulled up to the parking lot of the Blue Dog, I was shocked at the number of bikes there. Pretty much everyone from Outlaw Souls seemed to be here. It was well after last call, so I wondered what was going on.

I locked the car and went in. The place was filled with smoke and the only folks here were Outlaw Souls and Connie the bartender. She was off-duty and drinking from a bottle of Jack.

"Hey Ryder," she said as I walked in.

"Shut the fuckin' door," someone said. "We don't want no cops seeing we're here."

Like the four hundred bikes parked in front wouldn't give it away? Frankly, North La Playa police had more on their minds than busting us for drinking after the bar was closed.

I pushed my way to the back room where Hawk and Chalupa and Swole were.

"Where have you been, man? We've been here for hours," Swole said.

"Just as we thought, Las Balas thinks we blew up their warehouse," Hawk said. "We went and pulled everything out of ours and moved it to a different location."

Chalupa laughed. "They will never find it now."

"Where did we put it?" I asked. We didn't have a lot of shit, so it wouldn't be too hard to find a hiding place for the fifty or so crates of guns, ammo, and drugs we'd been keeping in the Public Storage locker.

"It ain't right, man," Swole said. "Not cool."

Now my curiosity was up. "Where is it?"

Chalupa was still grinning. "At the cemetery."

"The cemetery?"

"Yeah. In one of those mausoleum things."

"How the hell did we..." I shook my head. "Never mind. I have an emergency I'm dealing with and I need your help."

"What's the emergency?"

"Lily and her friend disappeared from the concert. If they ever made it there in the first place. They weren't at the meetup place after all the shit went down at the convention center."

"Tell me what happened. From the beginning," Hawk said.

So I did. When I got to the end, he shook his head. "It

makes no sense. No one is going to create a huge diversion at the convention center just to grab two teenage girls. Even if Las Balas did think we blew up their warehouse, there would be no reason to do that."

"Honestly, I'm less concerned with why and more concerned with where they hell they could be."

I needed to talk to that shit Scorpion, but couldn't get close to the warehouse because of all the cops. Where else could he be at this time of night? If he was with Lily, where would they be?

I had an idea. "I have something I need to do. You put some calls out, okay, Hawk?"

"You got it."

Twenty minutes later, I was parking the VW in a very empty parking structure near the Point. It was a long shot, and it was almost 3:00 am, but it was the only place I could think of that they might be.

The parking structure was well lit, even for this time of night, and the full moon illuminated the street once I walked out. I could hear seals barking from the ocean, and the normally busy tourist attraction was deserted.

There was no way they'd be here. Even still, it was worth a look. I ran across the street to the Ferris Wheel. It was next to closed food carts and stores with security gates up. "Lily?" I called. "Lily!"

My voice was lost in the slight mist coming off the ocean and I could still smell a slight bit of burning rubber from the warehouse fire.

Out of the corner of my eye, I saw something move. "Who's there?"

It was a slight flash from over near one of the buildings

and so I instinctively reached down to touch the gun inside my jacket pocket. "Who's there?" I asked again, more loudly.

I got close enough to see that it wasn't Lily, or any other female for that matter. It was a tall skinny guy wearing dark clothes. He was walking toward me, but his body language wasn't threatening.

"It's me. Scorpion." He'd been sitting on a bench next to the entrance to the Ferris Wheel.

"Where's Lily?" I demanded. "Where the fuck is my sister?"

"I don't know! I've been sitting here for two hours waiting for her. We were supposed to meet up here at one."

I wasn't even mad that Lily was planning on sneaking out of Paige's place to meet Scorpion. I was getting legitimately worried about the girls. This was not an instance of a couple of irresponsible teenagers coming home late from a concert.

"I've been texting her all night but they haven't been going through. I didn't know what else to do so I've just been sitting here."

"So you don't know anything about where they could be?"

"No! After the fire, the patches had a meeting but since I'm still prospecting I wasn't included, so I took off and came here."

Dammit. He was my one solid lead.

I turned to head back to the car. "Okay, thanks."

"Ryder?" Scorpion's hands were stuffed into his jeans pocket.

"Yeah?"

"Can I..." He cleared his throat. "Can I help you find her?"

This was no business for a Las Balas prospect to be involved in. I started to shake my head no, but he added, "Please? I just can't... I mean, I need to do something." He wiped his face with both hands. "I love her. What if...I..."

"Fine. You can come along with me. But you need to keep

your fucking mouth shut with anything you see or hear. Do you understand me?" This was probably a huge mistake, but my instincts were telling me that having him with me was better than leaving him to his own devices.

"Thank you, Ryder. I won't be in the way. I promise."

I shook my head and headed to the car with a tall, gangly, worried young man in tow.

We were driving up Berry Avenue and I was prepping Scorpion for what we were doing. "We're headed to the Blue Dog Saloon in North La Playa. I'd recommend taking off that fucking jacket and keeping your mouth shut. The brothers are not gonna be too happy if they find out who you are." I reached down and handed him a baseball cap. "Wear this and keep your head down."

"Scott," he said, as we passed by Swole's gym.

"What?"

"That's my name. Scott. Scorpion was just my nickname in high school."

"Did you graduate?"

"Yeah. I went to Fillmore. Was gonna go to LPCC but my ma got sick."

I didn't have time to ask more, so I just said, "There it is. Remember. Keep shut and let me do the talking." The more I thought about it, the more I was regretting bringing him along.

The place was still pretty packed despite the fact that it was almost 4:00 am. Hawk was gone, and of course Padre wasn't there. Neither was Yoda, but Chalupa saw us as soon as we walked in.

"Hey man, did you find..." He stopped dead in his tracks as soon as he saw Scorpion. He looked back and forth between us questioningly and then asked, "Any luck finding them?"

I shook my head and said "Nope. Where's Hawk?"

"I think he went over to Frog Park to talk to some guys. See if they heard anything."

I nodded and made my way to the back of the room and Scorpion kept his head down and followed us.

He did not go unnoticed, but no one bothered him because it was clear he was with me. I motioned for him to take the seat next to me, with our backs against the wall.

"So, *Scott*," I started. "Now would be a good time to tell me anything you know that might help me find my sister."

"Well. The only thing I know is that there was some talk about finding out who torched the warehouse and getting even."

"Okay. No surprise there. What else?"

"Not much. A couple of guys were running out to Baker to make a delivery for El Diablo tonight."

"What kind of delivery?"

He shook his head. "They don't tell me that kind of stuff."

My mind started to tickle with an idea, but it wasn't formed well enough to understand it yet. Before I got a chance to ask more, Hawk walked in and made a beeline for my table. "Ryder. I found out something that might help us find Lily."

PAIGE

As soon as she said, "Oh no, not you," my mom got up off the couch and ran into the bathroom and locked the door.

"What the hell?" I said, totally shocked. "What did she mean 'Not you too?'"

He shook his head and said, "First, what happened to you? Did you see a doctor?"

"No, it didn't get that far." I then told my dad the whole story. "It was terrifying."

He gave me a hug and said, "I know."

I looked at the bathroom door and said, "What's wrong with Mom?"

Dad just stood up and went to the bathroom door and knocked on it softly. "Rosemary? Honey?"

There was silence on the other side of the door as I sat there thinking this might be the weirdest night of my whole life. I half expected to wake up and discover that it had all been one really bizarre dream.

"Rosemary. I think it's time you told Paige what happened."

At first I didn't get it, but then it dawned on me like a kick in the gut. *"Oh no, not you too."* My mother had been attacked.

After what felt like an eternity, I heard the bathroom door unlock and the door opened. My mom came out and her eyes and nose were red from crying. I couldn't ever remember seeing my mother cry—not even when her own mother died.

"I think I will have that glass of wine."

I got up and poured her some of the wine into a plastic Starbucks cup. Her hands were shaking as she took it. "Thank you."

"Let me just say that I never wanted to tell you this. I'm not even sure I should be doing it now. But with your sister missing and... what happened to you... I don't know. It just seems like the right thing to do."

I didn't say a thing, but I waited.

"About seventeen years ago, your father was at the clinic and you were at school. The doorbell rang. I never answered the door, not even back then, but I could see a bouquet of flowers and I thought it might be from your dad. He and I... we were...well. I just thought he might be apologizing for something."

The affair, probably.

"As soon as I opened the door, the man pushed his way in and, well." She looked away.

"The whole thing was humiliating and degrading," my mom said. "There was a trial and I had to testify and everything."

"Where was I?" My mind was scanning back to when I was about 8 years old.

"You spent a lot of time with your Aunt Linda that summer. Remember?"

Oh my God, I remembered.

How awful! I had no idea my mother had gone through any of this. "My God, mom. I had no idea. Does Bailey know?"

They both shook their heads. "We never wanted to tell you girls. There have been too many secrets in this family." She put her face in her hands and started crying.

For the first time in my life, I saw my mother as a woman. Not as an authority figure or someone to judge me, but as a person.

I finally understood where I got the calling to help women came from. Even though I wasn't consciously aware of it, somehow I'd known that this issue was close to home.

The text message sound came from inside my purse, on my bed. I almost didn't hear it, but my mom looked at me and said, "Is that your phone?"

"Yeah. It could be Bailey," I said, walking to the bedroom door. *Or Ryder.* It was Ryder.

How's it going?

Weird. This has been a really strange night. Any word on the girls?

No. They were supposed to meet up with someone at the Point but never showed.

I had an instant flash of anger. They were supposed to meet someone at the Point? No, they were supposed to meet Ryder at Starbucks. It got me wondering about Lily and what kind of person she really was. No offense to Ryder, but Bailey didn't do shit like this.

Then again, how could I be sure? She'd snuck out of the house and got drunk at a party. Lord only knows what else she'd done that I didn't know about.

Hell, I didn't even know who her real father was until about ten minutes ago.

So we still don't know where they are?

No, but I'll keep you updated. Try and get some rest?

I don't think I'd be able to sleep. Besides, my parents are still here.

Go back home with them? I promise to let you know as soon as there's news.

I'll think about it. Thank you, Ryder. I appreciate everything you're doing.

YW

I wasn't surprised he just responded with "You're welcome." It was true, though. I really did appreciate the fact that he was out there looking for them. I had other things to deal with, namely my parents.

Putting the phone back in the charger, I grabbed the box of tissues I'd set by my bed when I'd fantasized about having sex with Ryder earlier. Was it really just earlier tonight?

I walked into the living room and saw my mom sitting on the couch with her head in her hands. "Hey. Here are some tissues."

She looked up and I saw mascara stains running down her cheeks as she took the box from me. "Thank you."

I sat down next to her, not really sure what to say.

"Dad says that you weren't hurt in the attack tonight. Physically, anyway."

"No, it was just some drunk asshole."

"I'm glad."

A moment passed and we both said, "I'm sorry" at the same time.

"You? Why are you sorry?" my mom asked.

"Because of what happened to you. You have been carrying this secret around for so long." As I looked at her, so many things made sense. Her overprotectiveness. Her trying so hard to keep Bailey and me from making mistakes.

"I guess I should have told you, but the time never seemed right."

"We need to find her, Paige," my dad added, "What time does the police station open? We can't just be sitting around here doing nothing."

Now it was my turn to be truthful. "Actually, I have some friends who are helping look for her."

"Friends? What kind of friends?" my mom asked.

"Well...the girl that Bailey went to the concert with... she is missing too. It's her older brother."

"What kind of help can another teenager do?" my dad asked. "This is a job for law enforcement."

"Her brother is the vice president of a motorcycle club and they were doing security for the concert."

"A *motorcycle gang?*" my mother said, a horrified expression on her face.

"Not a gang. A club. And, anyway, he's trying to track down what happened to his sister Lily and Bailey. They are well connected in La Playa and if there's information to find, I trust him to find it."

"How did you meet this man? Are you in the motorcycle club, too?" My mom was so clueless sometimes.

"I met him at work. As a customer."

"I don't understand how Bailey met him and his sister?"

"It's kind of a long story. Why don't we head back home and get some rest and I'll tell you in the car?"

"I thought we were going to the police?" my mom asked.

"Mom, the cops can't help us because she's only been missing for 12 hours. Ryder is looking for her right now. Why don't we let him work on things a bit longer? If we don't have news by noon, we'll file a missing persons report then. Okay? Let's go home so we can feed Betty White and let her out and wait for news there."

I sounded a lot more confident than I felt. But after the night we'd all had, I figured Ryder was right. Being at home in Verde Hills would feel a whole lot better than sitting in this apartment.

RYDER

I wanted to hear what Hawk had to say, but I really didn't want to talk about it in front of Scorpion, so I said, "Why don't you go take a leak? The bathrooms are right back there."

He nodded and got up and I wondered how such a skinny kid was prospecting with a violent MC like Las Balas. I also wondered what the hell Lily saw in him, because it sure wasn't his appearance. As soon as he walked away, Hawk leaned over to me and said, "You've got balls bringing a Las Balas recruit in here."

"It was the best of the worst options, trust me. So what's up?"

"Okay, so I went to Frog Park, where Viper and his guys do business. I asked if he knew anything about the explosion, the scare at the convention center, and anything about Lily's disappearance."

I didn't know what Hawk had to do to get that kind of information from one of our rivals and I didn't want to ask. The less I knew, the better. "What did he say?"

"He said that they didn't have anything to do with the

warehouse fire, and none of the other MCs in town were claiming it. Everyone thinks it was us."

"Of course they do, which puts us right in the middle of their target. What about the shots fired at the convention center? Was that them trying to get revenge?" That didn't make sense because of the short amount of time between the explosion and the shots at the convention center. They wouldn't have had time to get in.

"He said that it was most likely a false alarm. Like someone heard something they thought was gunfire, panicked, and then everyone started running."

"That makes sense. But none of this had anything to do with Lily. Who would kidnap her? It makes no sense." I hadn't really used the word "kidnap" to myself before this moment, but that was pretty much the only explanation at this point.

"Right. When I told him that the kid sister of one of our guys had gone missing, he said he didn't know anything about it. But when I pressed him, he changed his answer."

I could only imagine what he meant when he said, "pressed him."

"He said that El Diablo was making a delivery in Baker at an old airstrip out in the desert."

"That clearing off to the west?" That was a common place for planes to come in from South America and deliver and pick up drugs, guns...and sex trafficked girls.

"Fuck. But how would El Diablo get my sister? She was in the middle of a fucking crowd of 12,000 people."

"I don't even know that he has her, but it seems like we should take a little night ride out to make sure."

Before I could answer, I heard a commotion outside the bathroom. A bunch of guys were yelling and I heard banging on a wall.

I raced over there and sure enough, Scorpion was getting

his ass kicked. "Leave him alone!" I said in my loudest most commanding voice before physically pulling three guys off of him. They were drunk off their asses. "You need to go fucking home."

"What the fuck is he doing here? You brought a Las Balas guy here?" The guy talking was slurring his words.

Scorpion was wiping blood from his nose but nodded to me that he was okay.

"Last I checked I'm the VP of this club. When Padre isn't here, I'm the senior member and I don't need you questioning my fucking decisions."

"His sister is missing, man. The kid has been seeing her. He's here to help." Hawk stood by my side, in front of Scorpion in a protective stance.

"Help get information for Las Balas, you mean." The guy could barely stand up. It would take one punch to knock him out, flat on his ass.

"You want to start something? Is that what you want?" Honestly I hoped he would. I needed to beat the shit out of someone and I'd love nothing more than a good reason to do it.

"Come on, man. Let's go. My old lady is here and can drop you off at home."

They staggered out of the Blue Dog and I doubted they would even remember any of this in the morning. Looking out the window on the back door, I realized that the sky was getting lighter. It was already morning.

"Hey, kid. Let's take a little road trip."

I decided to take the bike since I could get there faster. It was about a hundred and ninety miles from La Playa to Baker, and it would take me a little over an hour to get there on my bike, versus almost two hours in the VW.

Hawk was rounding up the rest of the brothers—well, the ones who were sober enough to drive, anyway. A nice Sunday morning drive out to the desert was always appealing, even if the reason was an emergency.

Scorpion and I headed back to my apartment to get the bike.

"Why did you choose Las Balas, Scott?" We were stuck at a train crossing. He seemed like a pretty decent kid, all things considered. "There's a ton of other clubs in La Playa."

"One of my high school buddies was a prospect right out of school. They ran the neighborhood near Fillmore. I was gonna prospect then, but my ma got sick."

"What happened?"

"To the friend, or my ma?"

"Both."

"My friend got shot in a drive by and my ma died."

We were silent for a minute, as the train kept going past. I had to wonder if his friend was killed by one of our guys. Las Balas was one of our sworn enemies, and a lot of shit went down between us.

"I lost my parents, too. It sucks."

"Yeah. Lily told me. She said you've been real good to her, though. Stepped up like a dad and stuff. I didn't have any brothers or sisters, but I would have done it too, if I had."

"You don't really have a choice. You just do what you have to do. Family is family." The damn train finally passed and the gates went up.

"Look. You seem like a good kid, Scott. Can I give you some advice?"

"Sure."

"I know you think that you're in love with Lily. Shit, you might even really be. I don't know. But she's sixteen years old.

Being a patch in Las Balas isn't gonna lead you to any kind of life. You're gonna end up like your friend."

From his body language, I sensed defensiveness kicking in. "You gotta trust me here. If I could do it over again...if I could be twenty, I wouldn't do half the shit I did. If you and Lily are gonna pull through you need to do two things. First, wait until she's legal, man. Seriously. That shit will get you in prison. Second, stay the hell away from Las Balas. Go back to school or get a job or something. Go straight, get married—not to my sister—have a couple kids and take them to soccer practice. Choose a better life than this."

He was looking straight at me as I pulled into the parking structure of my apartment complex. "Is that what you want to do? Get out of Outlaw Souls? Choose a better life?"

I took a deep breath before getting out of the car. "I don't know, kid. Right now I just want to find my sister."

PAIGE

We got stuck at a stupid train on our way to the freeway. My mom was in the passenger seat and my dad was following behind in the Audi. My mom had thrown a shit fit when he got an R8. He kept saying he got a deal on it because he'd bought it for only $150,000 from another doctor in the office. Bailey called it his "mid-life crisis car."

I'd been surprised that they brought it to La Playa, but then again, my dad took it whenever they wanted to get somewhere in a hurry. It was a fantastic sports car. I'd only driven it a couple of times but was very glad he'd taught me how to drive a stick shift when I was in high school.

There wasn't much traffic on the road, but we were stuck at the damn train track. My mom looked completely drained as she rested her head back and had her eyes closed. The sun was coming up, and I wondered when the last time had been she'd pulled an all-nighter. I could barely remember the last time I'd stayed up to see the sunrise.

"Mom?"

"Hmmm?" she said, eyes still closed.

"Was it hard to love Bailey at first because of how she was

conceived?" It wasn't the kind of question you'd normally ask, but we were both tired and a little numb from the events of the night.

"Not at all. Not even for one minute. As soon as I found out I was pregnant, I saw it as a blessing from God. I didn't understand why He chose to bring Bailey into this world like that, but it was part of a plan that I didn't need to understand. When Mary got pregnant, she didn't understand it either. But she trusted. And as soon as I took one look at your sister's face, I knew. She was a pure, innocent baby. She deserved...deserves..." She started to cry and couldn't talk anymore.

I heard the Audi engine revving behind us and I reached out to squeeze her hand. "We'll find her, Mom. We just have to trust."

Betty White was barking her face off when we pulled in the driveway. Dad opened the garage door of the second garage and pulled the Audi in. It had only been a couple of weeks since I'd been here, but it felt like it had been months.

Mom got out of the car and went in the front door. Betty White came bounding out to greet me, sniffing and licking me. My parents had gotten her from a rescue place that my mom had done some charity work with through the club. She was some kind of mix but was all white and had blue eyes and had a black and pink nose and tongue. Bailey had named her when she became obsessed with the television show The Golden Girls on the oldies channel.

We walked in the huge double doors and it felt like I was walking back in time. I half expected Bailey to come bounding down the stairs, wearing her backpack and talking about some drama at school.

I wished I had a time machine and could go back to before the concert. I wanted to return to that simpler time when my only concern was whether or not to go to LBCs for burritos after the beach or not.

But those times were gone. I walked into the kitchen and set my stuff down on the island, looking out the window at the ocean view that was so expansive, you could see Margarita Island in the distance. Somewhere out there in the world was Bailey. If she could have come home, she would have. If she could have texted or called, she would have. But she hadn't done any of those things, and it was all I could do not to fall apart. I needed to stay strong for my parents.

"There are some bagels in the pantry if you're hungry," Mom said.

I shook my head. "I couldn't eat."

Dad walked in and said, "Let's remember to cancel tennis with the Schweigers."

"That's right. What should we tell them?"

"I don't care. Say we're sick or something." He went to get a bottled water.

"It wouldn't be far from the truth. None of us has slept all night and we are sick with worry."

"Have you heard from your friend yet? What was his name? Passenger or something?"

I checked my phone and saw that there was a missed call from Ryder. How did I miss the call? I quickly called back.

It rang three times before he picked up. "Ryder."

"Hey, it's Paige. Sorry I missed your call. Did you find the girls?" My heart was pounding, hoping he'd say yes. Both of my parents were looking at me expectantly.

"Not yet. But we got a solid lead. We are headed out to Baker now, I just stopped off to get my bike."

"Baker! That's halfway to Vegas! How could they have gotten all the way out there?"

"Oh my God," my mother said as she put her face in her hands and walked into the dining room.

"I'm not sure, actually. But we are all headed out there now. I'll let you know what we find."

"Okay."

I guess my fear came through my voice because he said, "I will find them. Paige. I will."

Tears came to my eyes and I nodded. "Be safe."

An hour later we were sitting in the den drinking coffee and trying to stay distracted. We had flipped through all of the television channels, but all that was on was another Guy Fieri food show, a bunch of church channels, and infomercials.

"Didn't you have some kind of business thing you wanted to talk about?" my dad said.

"Oh yeah. I did. I'm not sure this is the right time, though." I'd been up for more than twenty-four hours at this point.

"I can't think of anything better to talk about to take our minds off of everything, can you?" he said.

"No."

"Go ahead. We want to hear your idea."

"Okay. So, you know how I moved to La Playa because I wanted to help women and girls in some way, kind of like I did at the free clinic in Terrance."

"Right," they both said.

"Well, I've been applying for jobs like crazy at all of the nonprofits and things. I got one interview but they wanted someone with grant experience. Which was fine, because I want to be actually helping people and not in some office."

"Okay..."

"So my idea is to get a mobile health clinic that goes

around providing free or low-cost health services. Kind of like when Betty White got spayed at one of those mobile SPCA trucks."

"But you're not a doctor or a nurse," my dad said.

"No, but you are. I am imagining that the truck could go to parks and parking lots and people who wouldn't otherwise go to a doctor could come and get basic health care. We'd specialize in women's health."

My mom was nodding her head. "I think it's a great idea. Lindsey Shubert from the club just retired from being a nurse for 35 years at the hospital here. Healthcare has changed so much and is really inaccessible for a lot of people these days."

"What would be the costs involved? Where would you get the money?" my dad said.

"I don't have that information yet. I still need to do some research and a feasibility study."

"Honey, I love the idea. So many of the other doctors at our practice are fed up with the healthcare system. You put together a presentation and we can set up a meeting for you to pitch the idea to the partners."

"Thanks, Dad. I am really excited about this idea."

Well, I was excited about it earlier. I'd been excited about a lot of things.

RYDER

I had a lot of time to think on my way out to Baker. If you've ever driven or ridden from LA to Vegas or back, you've probably seen the giant thermometer off the freeway. The town of Baker had been a thriving pit stop for tired commuters for years. The Bun Boy restaurant had a pretty decent burger, and our club used to stop there on our Vegas runs. It shut down in 2013 because the owner refused to pay franchise fees to Bob's Big Boy. Well, that was the public story anyway. I heard that he was run out of town by bikers because he refused to pay them to stay away because they were scaring off the families.

Across the street was the abandoned Bun Boy Motel. It had always been a shitty place, but since it was abandoned it had become a hellhole for all kinds of illicit activities.

Scorpion was doing a good job of holding on to the back of my bike as we sped along. Having him with me definitely slowed me down, but something told me he would be useful to have around. Besides, he really did seem to care for Lily. Young love and all that shit.

Speaking of love...or something like it...the wide open

space of the desert got me thinking of Paige. I'd been thinking about her a lot these days. Too much, really. What if Sofia was right? What if this was my once chance at love again?

What kind of life could I offer a woman like her, though? She was having an adventure slumming in La Playa, but eventually she'd go back to her country club lifestyle. And where would that leave me?

I really didn't know how it could work out. She'd gone to college and came from money. I was a biker who worked in an auto shop. If she had half a mind, she'd run for the fucking hills and hook up with some lawyer named Biff or Lance or something.

She really did seem to have a pure heart, though, about wanting to help people. Who knows what can bring people together?

I didn't have much more time to think about it all, because we were getting close to Baker. Off in the distance, I could see a huge group of bikes congregating in the parking lot of the abandoned Bun Boy restaurant. It warmed my heart to see so many brothers coming out to help. I just hoped we weren't on some wild goose chase—or even worse, were too late.

My bike rumbled to a stop next to the Outlaw Souls. Everyone was there except for Yoda and Padre. It wasn't like Padre to not be here, but frankly, I had other things on my mind.

"What's the latest?" I asked Hawk.

He shook his head. "Nothing much. No one has seen El Diablo since yesterday morning, and a couple of his key guys are MIA, too."

"I think I might know something," Scorpion said. "I didn't pay much attention to it, but a couple nights ago, Chanclas and El Diablo were really drunk, and El Diablo was bragging that he was gonna show every MC in La Playa who was boss. Said that everyone in town would fear him and shit like that. Chanclas asked what he meant and he said something about being two fewer souls in Outlaw Souls. I just thought it was trash talk."

"Who is Chanclas?" I asked. I thought I knew all of the Las Balas patches.

"He came from downtown LA. Didn't have to prospect. They just brought him right in."

That made me wonder who he was targeting. Two fewer Outlaw Souls? Maybe I ought to be more concerned about Padre than I was. "Do you have any idea where they could be?"

"Well, the first month or so I was prospecting, they had me drive a U-Haul full of boxes down to an old water tower out here."

"There's a couple of them," Hawk said, nodding to the tall structures in the distance.

"It was the furthest one from the road. As soon as I arrived with the truck, they made me leave. I walked back to the highway and someone gave me a ride back to La Playa."

"Well, none of this may have anything to do with where Lily is, but I definitely would like to have a conversation with El Diablo." I turned to Hawk and said, "Whaddya say you and I take a little ride out to the water towers and see if we can find him?"

"Sounds good, brother." Hawk then turned to Swole and said, "Swole, can you keep an eye on the kid, here?"

"Why, because I'm a woman?" she asked, grinning.

"You're a woman?" he said. "I never noticed."

"Fuck you," she said, laughing.

"You wish," Hawk replied.

They were busy bantering, and I was busy figuring out how I was going to get El Diablo to tell me where my sister was. I just knew he had something to do with her disappearance.

We'd gone to the first water tower, but no one was there. I was glad it wasn't July because it gets up close to 130 out here. They don't call it Death Valley for nothing.

"Let's head out to the other water tower and see if he's there." Without waiting for an answer, Hawk left me in the dust.

About half a mile up a narrow dirt road set among cacti and bushes was the second tall water tower in the Baker area. From a distance I could see two bikes and felt confident that it was El Diablo and that guy Chanclas.

The closer we got, the more my confidence melted like ice cream on a 130 degree day. The first bike was El Diablo's all right. I'd recognize it anywhere. But the second bike was also one I'd recognize anywhere—from my own workplace. It belonged to Padre.

My first instinct was to think that maybe Padre had been taken hostage by El Diablo. But as I approached, I saw that they were standing side by side talking. Padre was here of his own free will.

As soon as El Diablo heard us, he jumped on his bike and raced off. Hawk waved at me and followed El Diablo, leaving me alone in the middle of the desert with Padre.

My bike slowed to an idle. "What are you doing here, Padre?"

He looked sad and old as he shook his head. "This wasn't supposed to happen."

"You didn't mean to come out here? How did you get here, Padre?" I was getting concerned. He wasn't making sense.

"I rode here." He shook his head again. "It wasn't supposed to happen. He was only supposed to scare you."

"Scare me? Who was supposed to scare me?" I really wished I knew what the hell he was talking about.

"El Diablo. I didn't mean for him to..."

The reality of what was going on started to seep into my brain, but it couldn't accept it. "Tell me what is going on, Padre."

"You were stealing from me, and..."

"I wasn't stealing from you," I corrected, "but go on."

"And I wanted you and the others to know that disloyalty is punished. El Diablo owed me a favor from that time with the cops and I called it in. I told him to grab Lily and just hold her for an hour or two. When you discovered her missing, then you'd learn a lesson in loyalty."

The rage that rose inside of me was sudden and fierce. The man I considered a father figure after my parents had died betrayed me by hiring some thug—a sex trafficker—to kidnap my little sister as a lesson. I was going to kill him.

I lunged off my bike and reached out to grab his neck. I had weapons, but I wanted to feel him choke under my hands.

"Ryder! I didn't mean it. He was supposed to bring her back. I swear!" His eyes were wild with fear but I didn't care. Punches started landing on his old face.

"You motherfucker. You gave my baby sister to a fucking sex trafficker and believed him when he said he'd bring her back? You're as stupid as you are old."

Padre wasn't fighting back but was in a defensive posture with his arms up. "That's why I came out here. To get him to release her. I went to the warehouse last night to try and stop him."

I stopped punching him. "Wait. You were at the warehouse? When?" We were at the concert last night. I saw him at the convention center.

"When you guys were all inside. I said I had to take a leak..."

Oh my God. "So you started the explosion?"

"Yes, it was supposed to be a couple of little explosives. Just to distract him so he wouldn't kidnap Lily. I changed my mind and didn't know what to do."

I wanted to start kicking him, but it's no relief to beat a defenseless old man, so I stopped. "Where is she, Padre? Where is my goddamn sister?"

"I don't know! He just said he had her and another girl hidden away until sunset and then the plane from Colombia would come to take them."

That meant we had about five hours to find Lily and Bailey before they were transported to South America to God knows what fate.

I grabbed Padre by the collar of his jacket. "If I don't get my sister back, I am going to kill you personally. I will fucking kill you."

"I know. I'm so sorry, Ryder. So sorry."

"Sorry doesn't mean shit. Get my sister back."

PAIGE

My eyes were involuntarily closing as I sat on the couch with my parents. My cell phone was clutched in my left hand and I kept checking it every two minutes, hoping to hear from Ryder.

"Honey, why don't you go up to your room and get some rest?" my mom said.

"No, I'm okay."

"You most certainly are not okay," my dad said. "You're passing out. How long have you been awake?"

"Twenty-eight hours."

"That's it. You're getting some rest." My mom stood up and extended her hand. "Give me the phone. I'll watch it to see if we get any calls."

"No, really. It's…"

"Paige Melissa. Listen to your mother."

"Okay. But I'll keep the phone." I had a password set and really didn't want my parents snooping around my phone. Ryder and I had activated each other on Find My Friends on our cell phones and I wanted to be able to track where he was while he was looking for our sisters.

"I'll lie down, but only for an hour or so." I headed toward the stairs. "You guys should take your own advice. It's been a long night for all of us."

Fifteen minutes later, I was lying on the full-sized bed in the bedroom I'd grown up in. It seemed like a lifetime ago that I stared at the NSYNC posters and dreamed of being a veterinarian. Instead, I was a waitress who couldn't get another job.

"Shit!" I'd forgotten that I was supposed to work this afternoon. I grabbed the phone and called work.

"Tiny's," barked the voice on the other end of the line.

"Martha, it's Paige."

"Yeah?" Martha Jiminez was a woman of few words.

"Look. I'm having a bit of a family emergency and I can't come in for my shift."

"And by 'family emergency' you mean you were at that concert last night?"

"No. It's...it's my sister. She's missing."

"Oh. Well, that's different. I can get Rocky to work a double. Keep us posted, okay?" Her voice sounded strange when she was being empathetic. It was like she didn't know how to do it.

"Thanks, Martha. I will."

I barely had time to hang up the phone before sleep overtook me.

When I woke up, my mind forgot what was happening and my body remembered being in my childhood bed. My eyes were closed and I could smell the familiar scent of pancakes and bacon coming from the kitchen. I could hear kids playing outside on their bikes and the sounds of a ballgame on TV.

I was just a carefree teenager, sleeping in on a Sunday afternoon. Bailey was probably in her room...

Bailey! The reality came flooding back to me. Bailey was missing and I was lying here in my bed dreaming of pancakes. What was wrong with me?

I grabbed my phone and my heart sank. No messages from Ryder.

"That's it." I sat up and smoothed my hair. "I'm going out there. I'm not going to sit around here like some teenager. I may not be able to do much, but it's better than sitting around here."

"Won't you at least eat before you go?" My mom was stress cooking. She'd made pancakes and bacon, blueberry muffins, lemon scones, and was now in the middle of making a chocolate cake. "I just need to keep busy," she'd said when I raised my eyebrows at the buffet in the kitchen.

"I don't think I can eat, Mom."

"Take a few muffins. The girls are likely to be hungry when you pick them up."

I didn't have the heart to tell her that there was a real possibility that I wouldn't be bringing them home. She didn't know the kind of people we were dealing with.

One look at my dad's face and I could tell that he understood. He stood up and walked over to the desk in the living room and grabbed a set of keys. "Take the Audi, Paige. You'll get there faster."

Dad was right. The R8 was such an amazing machine that I barely felt the 110 miles an hour I was going. The stretch of highway on the way to Baker was deserted this time of day, and if I did happen to get pulled over, I'd explain that my sister was missing and ask for a police escort. But pretty much everyone sped along this part of the desert.

Feeling the engine rev as I switched gears, I thought of Ryder. It was no wonder he'd fallen in love with motorcycles. Being the one in control of a powerful engine definitely helped when you felt out of control in life. He'd gotten into it when his parents were killed, and I was feeling it now, worried about Bailey and Lily.

It was shocking, really, how quickly Ryder had become part of my everyday life. I found myself thinking about him all the time. I'd smile when I remembered something funny or witty he said, and my heart lifted every time he walked into Tiny's. I'd only lived in La Playa a few weeks, but in that short time, that hunk of a man had wormed his way into my life.

As I wrapped my hand around the gear shift, I found myself looking forward to getting my hands on Ryder. It had been a long time since I'd been with a man, and I was long overdue for some loving.

Was it really love, though? We didn't exactly run in the same circles. I couldn't really imagine bringing him to the club or having dinner with my parents. I had to grin imagining him at the Schweigers' summer barbecue. "So, Ryder? What do you do for a living? You're a mechanic? And a biker? How interesting. I think I see someone I need to speak to."

I didn't see any way that Ryder and I could have a long-term future. He didn't strike me as the kind of guy who wanted 2.5 kids and a big house, complete with driving carpool and Girl or Boy Scouts.

Would I be willing to give all of that up to be with him?

My phone dinged with a text message. I changed lanes and then pulled off to the side of the road to read it. There was no way I was risking an accident in my father's $150,000 car.

Lots to tell you when I see you but no word yet on the girls. I know who has them and why, but not where. I'll text when I know more.

I sat there for a moment and wondered if I should tell him I was on my way. No, he'd probably tell me not to come. Turn around and wait at home. But he wouldn't say that if I were already there.

Putting the car in gear, I turned the radio on. In about an hour, I'd be one step closer to finding my sister.

RYDER

I was so pissed off I was shaking. Of all the things I could have imagined, Padre being responsible for Lily's disappearance was not even on my radar. The only reason I didn't kill him right then and there was because I figured I'd have a better shot of getting her back alive if I didn't. But, so help me God, if one hair on my sister's head—or Bailey's, for that matter— was harmed, I would kill that motherfucker with my bare hands.

The guy was obviously losing it mentally, because the man I knew would never have done something like this. His judgment was clearly way off. But that was a different issue for another day. Right now, I had five hours to find my sister, otherwise I'd be spending the rest of my life in South America trying to find her there.

I headed back to the Bun Boy parking lot to see if Hawk had any luck chasing down El Diablo. When I got there, the whole damn place had turned into some kind of tailgating party. The clubs had supposedly come to "help," but instead were drinking and smoking weed, blasting music, and basically partying.

Fortunately, the Outlaw Souls were taking it seriously, and when I pulled up to the corner where everyone was gathered, I found Scorpion, Swole, Trainer, and Chalupa looking at a map of the nearby desert.

"Hey Ryder. I'm guessing you had no luck?" Chalupa asked.

"Where's Hawk?" Scorpion wondered.

I wasn't really sure how to answer that. Did I tell them that I'd found Padre and that he was responsible for this whole mess?

I didn't want to, but I pretty much had to.

I paused for a moment, thinking about how to say it. "I didn't find Lily or Bailey, but I did make a very upsetting discovery."

"Oh my God, no..." Trainer said. "Not..."

"No, no. Not that. When we got to the water tower, we saw two bikes there. One was El Diablo and as soon as he heard us, he took off. Hawk followed him."

"Who was the other bike?" Swole asked.

"It was Padre."

"Padre! What was he doing there? Why didn't he ride with us?"

"Wait. Was he kidnapped too?"

I shook my head. "No. He was behind the whole thing. He thought I was stealing parts from the garage and decided to call in a favor with El Diablo and have him grab Lily for a couple of hours to scare me and teach me a lesson about loyalty, but it blew up."

"That's fucked up, man," Trainer said.

Swole shook her head. "I can't believe that. He told you that himself?"

"Yeah. He came out here to find Lily and make it right, but El Diablo has a plane coming after dark to take them to South America."

"What the actual fuck?" Chalupa was in total shock.

"I know. So that means we have less than five hours to find them."

Scorpion grabbed the big paper gas station map and handed it to me. "Here's a map of the area, and we circled anything that could be a place where they could hide two girls."

"Obviously, they could be in the back of a van parked out in the middle of the desert, but it will give us some organization as we look," Trainer said.

"What about those guys?" I asked, nodding to the other MCs who were laughing and drinking. "Do we get them in on it?"

Chalupa shook his head. "I wouldn't. The more people we have out there, the more likely they are to move the girls. Maybe the party in the parking lot will be a good diversion for Las Balas to think we aren't looking."

I nodded. "Makes sense."

Just then, Hawk roared into the parking lot. He swung off his bike and took off his helmet. "He took off. I tried to follow him, but he went behind a huge hill and by the time I got there, he'd disappeared."

"Shit. Okay, let's spread out and canvass the area. You guys update Hawk about what happened with Padre, and let's leave one at a time, spaced out every five minutes so we don't draw attention from us all leaving at the same time." I grabbed my helmet. "I'll go first, and text you in about an hour. I'll take this area here," I said, pointing to the desert across the street from us.

"Padre? What happened to Padre?" Hawk asked.

If I had to tell the story again I'd probably puke, so I just left.

I was getting frustrated. Here I was on what would be a beautiful Sunday afternoon riding my bike in the California desert. But instead of listening to some tunes and feeling the wind in my face as I straddled a powerful machine, riding with my brothers on the way to Vegas, I was wandering around the desert like some fucking nomad looking for my little sister.

I knew I should update Paige, but what was I going to say? *Oh, hey, yeah, sorry. My boss is delusional and thought I was stealing fifty-dollar parts from him, and so he arranged for our sisters to be kidnapped by sex traffickers.* It was better that she knew nothing than to know that.

I'd been riding around for forty-five minutes and hadn't seen a damn thing. No vans parked anywhere. No structures where the girls could be held. Maybe they were being held in a nearby city or something? They wouldn't go as far as Vegas because the Metro Police there were on top of things. There'd be no way for an unauthorized plane to get anywhere near Vegas air space, either.

If I were going to hide someone, where would I go? I sat with my bike idling and realized I was going to need fuel soon. Maybe I'd head back into town and get some gas before...

"Wait. Holy shit. It was right in front of my face the whole time." I turned around and headed to the abandoned Bun Boy Motel.

PAIGE

As I approached the city of Baker I saw "the world's largest thermometer," which was a huge tourist attraction back in the day. I'm pretty sure there is an old photograph of Bailey and me standing in front of it during one of our trips to Las Vegas.

Those were some amazing memories. Every few years, we'd stay at Circus Circus and while my mom took her chances in the casino, my dad gave Bailey and me each a roll of quarters and let us go crazy in the arcade. Once our stash had run out, we'd go see the circus acts.

Tears began to sting my eyes as I remembered those days. We had to find Bailey. We just did.

I stole a quick glance at my phone to see if Ryder had written with an update yet. He hadn't. The last thing he said to me was "stay at home where you're safe." Of course, I hadn't. But I wasn't ready to just show up. "Hi everyone. Here I am in my dad's expensive sports car and I want to help."

Speaking of which, as soon as I drove by the huge gathering of bikers in the old Bun Boy parking lot, I realized it might have been a mistake to bring this car. Not only did it attract a lot of attention, but my dad would kill me if anything happened to it.

It made more sense to park the car in a somewhat private location and then walk over to where the Outlaw Souls were meeting up.

I looked around and noticed that the Bun Boy Motel across the street had been shut down, and that seemed like a good place to park. I'd tuck the car over in a spot that was visible to me so I could keep an eye on it, but wasn't like I was roaring into a parking lot in a showy sports car.

As I was parking the car, my heart leapt as I heard my phone ding with a text message. Unfortunately, it was just my dad.

How's it going? Any luck?

I just got here, Dad. I promise I'll let you know.

Okay. Your mom and I love you both.

As tough as this was on me, this had to be a hundred times harder on them.

I love you, too.

I hid the car as best I could while still keeping it where I could see it. I was crossing the parking lot when I heard a weird noise coming from the building. It was like a weird banging vibration. Since it wasn't a windy day, I figured I'd go investigate before heading across the street to the Bun Boy.

The closer I got, the more it sounded like it was coming from the metal railing that led up to the second floor of the motel.

Why would the stair bannister be clanging and vibrating? I leaned over and put my ear on it, and decided to follow the sound/vibration upstairs.

Although the motel was abandoned, it was still in pretty good shape. The downstairs windows were boarded up and there was graffiti everywhere. Empty beer cans and vodka bottles lay alongside syringes and whatnot. It just looked like a typical abandoned building.

It was a little creepy, but nothing too bad. It was broad daylight and I didn't see any other cars or bikes around. All of the activity seemed to be going on across the street. It was really just curiosity that was prompting me to explore. I couldn't imagine what would make such a strange sound.

I got to the top of the stairs and noticed that these windows hadn't been boarded up, but had raggedy curtains that were all closed. I was half tempted to keep exploring, but figured I'd better get back downstairs where I could see the car and go find Ryder.

Suddenly, I heard a thump come from one of the rooms. I stood frozen for a moment. I was half tempted to run downstairs to safety. But I also wanted to know what it was. What if it was Bailey?

As I stood there, I heard it again. Thump, clang.

Following the sound, I went up to the room that was right in the middle of the outdoor hallway. The tattered curtain was closed, but I figured I might be able to see in if I pressed my face against the glass.

Peering in, it was hard to see because the glass was dirty, the view was obscured by the curtains, and the inside of the room was dark. I sat there for a minute and didn't see anything, so I figured it was just my dramatic imagination getting the best of me.

Before I could turn around, though, someone yanked my ponytail, pulling me back into them. I didn't even have a chance to fight them off. Strong, leather jacket clad arms wrapped around me and a hand came over my face with a cloth and pressed it against my mouth and nose.

I began kicking and trying to scream, but the cloth had some kind of alcohol or something on it. I was squirming and trying to get loose and his leg swept under mine, making me lose my balance.

The last thing I was aware of as the world turned dark was me falling limp into a stranger's arms.

The next thing I noticed was that my head was pounding with a headache. It felt like Charlie Watts from the Rolling Stones was going to town inside my brain. My mouth was dry, too.

I tried to open my eyes, but my eyelids were so heavy I couldn't. It felt like I was on the floor, on a carpet. My hands were tied behind my back and my legs seemed to be tied up, too. I heard male voices, speaking softly.

"What the fuck was I supposed to do, Diablo? She was right there, sticking her face in the window. She had to have seen them."

"Why didn't you just leave her in the desert? Now we have three people we need to deal with. The Garcia brothers are only expecting two people. Besides, she's a little old." That came from the guy called Diablo.

"Look, I know she's no teenager, but she's blond and American. That has to be worth something. Why don't you ask the Garcia brothers if they want her? If not, then I'll have some fun with her and then dump her in the desert."

My heart froze in panic. They were talking about me!

The Diablo guy was silent for a moment, apparently contemplating the idea. It was then that I heard soft whimpering coming from the other side of the room.

"You shut up!" the second guy said. "I told you both to stay the fuck quiet."

After what felt like forever, the Diablo guy said, "Fine. Come with me and we'll go down to where we get reception and I'll call. If I can't get at least a thousand for her, you can have her. I highly doubt they're gonna want some chick in her thirties."

In my thirties? If I weren't in this position, I'd be offended. I was only twenty-five!

"I'm getting ten grand each for the teenage girls. I said they were virgins, though." The Diablo guy laughed and his companion joined them.

"Too bad. I wouldn't mind giving them a little going away present."

"Don't fucking touch them. You can have the old one if he says no."

Their footsteps crossed right next to my head as they walked to what I assumed was the door.

"You both stay fucking quiet. I don't know what you did to get her attention, but if it happens again, you will be very, very sorry."

I waited until I heard the door close and the footsteps walking down the stairs before I tried to speak.

"Hey," I said softly. My voice sounded hoarse.

"Paige? Is that you?" Bailey whispered. "We're blindfolded and can't see anything but we heard them drag someone in."

I forced my eyes open, but all I could see was a sliver of light reflecting on a popcorn ceiling. "Oh my God, Bailey! I'm so glad you're all right. Is Lily okay, too?"

"Yeah. I'm okay. My shoulders hurt from being tied up."

I rolled over and saw her tied to a chair. "I was banging the chair against the sink to make noise."

"That was smart. I heard it and that's why I came upstairs."

There was a moment of silence and then Bailey said, "Paige, I'm scared."

"Me, too," said Lily.

"What's going to happen to us?" Bailey asked.

"I don't know, guys. But I can tell you one thing. I am not leaving your side. There are people looking for you and they will find us."

"I don't know who did this, that's the thing. We got out of the car a few blocks from the convention center so we could look at T-shirts and stuff. We were talking to this kid and the next thing we knew this big SUV pulls up and these guys get out and grab us and drag us inside."

"We didn't even have time to fight!" Lily said.

"I heard the kid yelling. 'Hey stop' but we drove away."

"So you never even made it to the concert?"

"No! I bet it was amazing." Poor Bailey sounded distraught. "We had floor seats and everything."

"Actually, the concert was interrupted. Billie Eilish did her set and then there were some kind of gunshots or something right after MCR went on."

"What?" they both asked.

"They weren't really gunshots but everyone panicked and started running. They had to cancel the show."

"Oh my God, how weird."

"The good news is, maybe they'll reschedule and we can still see them," Bailey said.

My sister, ever the optimist. I didn't want to remind her that if she were sold to sex traffickers in South America, not seeing My Chemical Romance in concert would be the least of her problems.

I just needed to formulate a plan to get us out of here before that Diablo guy came back.

RYDER

I was just about to turn into the Bun Boy Motel parking lot when I got a text. It was from Hawk.

Padre just showed up. I think you better get here.

OMW.

Since it was only across the street, it took me two minutes to get there. What I found when I arrived was disturbing to say the least. Padre was there, physically, but he wasn't acting like himself. He was backed up against the back door to the Bun Boy Restaurant, and his eyes were dark and wild. He was brandishing a knife and yelling.

"Get away from me. Where's my wife? What did you do with my wife?"

"Padre. She's not here," Chalupa said.

"Why are you calling me that? My name is Paul. I don't know what you want from me. My wife and I are on our way to Las Vegas and we stopped here for dinner. We always stop here for dinner before we go see Tom Jones and Siegfried and Roy. Nancy will kill me if we miss the show."

Clearly he was having some kind of psychotic break. Tom Jones hadn't performed in Vegas since the 1980s. I really didn't have time to deal with this now. I had less than three hours to find Lily and Bailey.

"Paul," I said, stepping forward. "No one wants to hurt you or Nancy. You can put the knife away."

He looked crazily around at us. "I don't know who any of you people are. I just want to find my wife, have dinner, and get to Las Vegas."

"I'm sure your wife just went to the ladies' room. You know how long they take in there, right?"

His shoulders loosened a bit. "Right. Yeah, you're probably right. She is always in there chatting with all the women like they're best friends."

"Exactly. Who knows what they're talking about? My friend Susie will go in the bathroom and look for her, okay?"

I nodded to Swole who said, "Yeah. Sure. I'll go see if I can find Nancy in the ladies' room." She walked around the corner to where the front door of the abandoned restaurant was.

"My friend Pedro here will take you back to your car, okay?" I motioned to Hawk. "Do you remember where you parked your car?"

Padre looked confused for a minute and then said, "I think it's in the parking lot in the back."

"Okay, Pedro will take you to your car, and Susie will bring your wife Nancy out and you guys can still make it to Vegas in time to see Tom Jones, okay?"

He nodded and turned toward the parking lot. "Just take him to his car and wait with him, okay? I need to check out the motel across the street."

"Okay. Will do. Be safe."

"Can I come with you?" Scorpion said as he walked alongside me. "I hate just sitting here doing nothing."

I shook my head. "Look, kid. I don't even know what I'm going to find over there. It's probably nothing. What would really help me would be for you to keep your ears open to see what the other MCs are saying. Since you're a recruit for Las Balas, they won't think twice about talking around you."

He looked dejected. "Okay."

I didn't have time to talk anymore. Something was telling me to get over to that motel, and quick.

Two minutes later I entered the parking lot of the abandoned motel. My eyes caught on a shiny black Audi parked under a tree behind a dumpster. "What the hell?"

I parked my bike and walked over there. It looked like the R8 that I'd seen at Paige's place when I dropped her off the other night. Sure enough, the license plate said DrAntn. Why would Paige's dad be here, and why was his car behind the dumpster? Was he looking for Bailey?

I decided to go explore the motel. The lower level was all boarded up, but the upper level wasn't. Maybe the girls were in one of the rooms.

As I walked through an opening toward the back stairs, passing a broken out vending machine, I could hear voices. Actually, it was just one guy and he was talking in Spanish. Despite having lived in La Playa all this time, I didn't know Spanish. But the closer I got, the more I realized I knew who was talking. El Diablo. He was standing next to that guy Chanclas and he was on the phone.

My fists clenched and I wanted to run out and kick the shit out of him. But I couldn't do that because then he'd just move the girls. If they were even here, that is.

Instead, I tiptoed around to the side of the building, making sure to stay in the shadows so I wouldn't be seen.

I took the side stairs up to the second level and slowly made my way up to each window. I peeked in as best I could to see if anyone was in them. The first three rooms were clearly empty. But the one in the middle—I wasn't so sure. I thought I could hear muffled voices coming from inside.

Pressing my face up against the window I tried to make out what was inside. Yes, there were definitely people in there. I closed my eyes so I could hear better and pressed my ear up. Then, I heard it. Lily! Lily was in there and she was probably talking to Bailey. My heart soared. She was alive!

Now I just had to figure out what to do. With El Diablo and Chanclas right below me, I couldn't make too much noise. I needed to find a way to get in the room, get the girls out, and take them to a safe place.

I crouched down below the railing so that El Diablo wouldn't see me. That also meant that I couldn't see them. I just needed to think. I could break the window but that wouldn't help. Maybe if I got their attention somehow they could open the door. No, they were probably tied up or else they'd just open the door themselves.

There was only one door and one window in. My time was running out, because I heard El Diablo and Chanclas walking toward me.

"Just as I thought, the Garcia brothers don't want the old one. You can have her. Do what you want and then dump her in the desert. Just make sure she can't identify us. Got it?"

"Oh yeah, brother. I got it." His voice sounded gleeful. "I'm gonna have me some blond pussy tonight!"

He was disgusting. Who was he talking about, the old one? Could it be Paige's mother? No. She wouldn't be here. Then, suddenly it hit me. The car. Paige probably borrowed her dad's car and came down. "The old one" was Paige!

Goddamn it. Instinctively I stood up to look in the window again. It wasn't my smartest move, because as soon as I stood up, my head exploded in pain and the world closed into darkness.

PAIGE

As soon as we heard someone at the window, we all froze. We'd been talking softly about how to escape, but then heard someone outside the door.

"Shh," I whispered. If it were that Diablo guy, he'd have just come inside. Lord only knows who else would be there. If it were a friend, yelling for help would work. But if it were a foe, we might make things worse.

Before I had a chance to do anything, there was a thud, and then the sounds of someone being dragged. This was not good. We needed to get out of here immediately. From what I could tell by the angle of the sun coming through the curtain, it was late evening, and the sun would soon be going down. Whatever they planned to do, my guess was they planned to do it at night.

As soon as the sounds of dragging went away, I twisted myself into a sitting position. "Maybe if we sit back to back, Bailey, we can untie each other's hands. Like that game Mom did at your 13th birthday party?"

"Okay."

I scooted over to where she was and managed to get up

on the bed, and we sat back to back. I started fumbling with the rope but couldn't feel where the knots would untie.

"I know," Lily said. "I can look at what you're doing and give verbal directions." She scooted over to where we were and started talking.

"Okay, Paige, just to the left of your thumb is the main loop of the knot on Bailey's wrist. If you take two fingers and loosen it... No, put your finger right between those...yeah. Like that."

My arms were absolutely killing me and I vowed that if I got out of this I would spend whatever money I needed to get a nice massage. But with Lily's instructions, we were getting each other's ropes loosened. It was working!

It took almost an hour, but finally my rope was loosened enough to slip my hands out. The skin was bloodied and torn, but my hands were free. It wasn't as easy to untie my feet as they make it look in the movies, and I still had to spend another twenty minutes getting the girls untied too. Eventually, though, we got it.

"Okay, now what do we do?" Bailey asked. "We can't exactly walk out the front door."

I went into the bathroom and noticed that the window in there was one of the older ones that would be big enough to crawl through. Thank God it wasn't one of those tiny shower ones with vented glass.

The thing was, the window was sealed shut from years of disuse and the only way out was to break the glass. Not only were we risking getting cut, but it would make a noise.

"Okay. Look. Down there is Dad's car. See that? We can take one of the curtains, smash the window, and then climb out and down that tree and run to the car."

Bailey and I knew full well how to climb down trees and sneak out, but what about Lily? "Do you think you can do it?"

She nodded yes, so I went into the main room and yanked

down a thick curtain from the rod and dragged it into the bathroom. The place had been stripped of anything else like towels or sheets, so this was all we had to work with.

"We have to be ready to scramble out the window the second we get the opening big enough, Okay?"

The girls nodded. I held the curtain up over the window.

"Okay. One...two...three!"

I kicked the window as hard as I could to break it, but nothing happened except it made a really loud sound.

So I kicked again and heard a small crack. So much for my Charlie's Angels moves. "Help me!"

All three of us started kicking the shit out of the window until finally it shattered.

"Bailey. You go first. Lily, watch how she does it."

I wrapped Bailey up in the curtain until she was safely through the opening and then took it back in when she reached the tree. Bailey slid down the tree like a fire pole. It probably hurt like hell, but at least she was free.

Lily was next and I was surprised at how quickly she moved. She was out and down the tree in less than a minute.

Now it was my turn. At twenty-five it had been a long time since I'd snuck out any windows. It took me a couple minutes longer, but also because I was wrestling with the damn curtain. Finally, I got out, but I could feel blood dripping somewhere. Whatever, I didn't have time to look.

Shimmying down the tree was no small feat, either, and I made a note to get to the gym more often.

As soon as my feet touched the ground, I was ready to run to the car.

Except for one little problem. I was staring down the end of a gun being held by a guy standing two feet from me. Where the hell did he come from? Behind him, two other guys were holding Bailey and Lily.

Dammit! We were so close.

"What the fuck do you think you're doing?" This must be that Diablo guy, because his voice sounded the same. "You think you are going to steal from me? Those girls represent twenty thousand dollars." He took a step forward and said, "You, on the other hand, are a worthless puta. I should fucking kill you right now."

I started hyperventilating and felt sheer panic. This was how I was going to die?

"Diablo, man. Come on. You said I could have her." That was the other voice from the room. I looked at him and he was a greasy fat guy who looked to be about forty.

Diablo stood holding the gun in my face, and then took a step backward.

"Fine. Get the bitch out of my face then. I don't want to see her."

At that command, the guy came over and grabbed my arm as the girls were wrestled into the same SUV that they were probably brought here in. "Come on ,girls. We have a plane to catch."

RYDER

The first thing I noticed was a ringing in my ears. It was loud and high-pitched, like feedback between a microphone and a speaker. The next thing, of course, was a cracking headache and the awareness that my face was in the dirt.

Where was I? What had happened? I had to strain my brain to put the pieces together. I was outside laying in dirt. Why? That's right. I rode out to the desert. I came here to find Lily. I found her and...I must have been hit over the head and dragged somewhere.

I tried opening my eyes, but all I saw was darkness. Was I blind? No. It was just night and pitch black.

Night! Dammit. I need to get to the water tower before that plane comes. I assumed that whoever hit me over the head had already moved the girls and Paige by now. I needed to get up and find my bike.

Trying to lift my head up was like doing a pushup with Shaquille O'Neal standing on my back. I wondered if I had a concussion or something. That damn ringing in my ears!

Even still, I didn't have time to worry about that. I needed to get to my bike. I made it to standing, but was hit with a wave of intense dizziness. Bending over at the knees, I took a few deep breaths. "You can do this, Ryder."

I patted around in my jacket for my phone, but it was gone. All I had on me were my bike keys and the hair tie from Gerard Way. What a strange combination of things to have in an emergency.

I'd left my bike over by Russell's car, but first I needed to figure out where I was. They couldn't have dragged me too far, so chances were I was still pretty close to the motel.

Sure enough, there it was, about a hundred feet behind me. My boots crunched the gravel as my eyes got adjusted to the darkness. I sure the hell hoped I wasn't too late. There was no way of knowing what time it was or how long I'd been unconscious. The moon was just starting to rise, which meant that it hopefully was still early.

As I got close enough to where I'd left my bike, I noticed that the car was still there, too. I wasn't sure if that was good news or bad news. I also saw some broken glass and a curtain laying on the ground near a tree that hadn't been there before.

Across the street, the party appeared to have died down. I thought about going over and rounding up the rest of the Outlaw Souls to help me out by the water tower, but frankly, I didn't want to waste the time. This was something I was going to have to do on my own.

I rode like a bat out of hell across the desert toward that water tower. Seriously, I was going so fast that my bike actually caught air a few times. The whole time, I just kept praying that I wasn't too late and that I'd get there in time to stop El Diablo from loading Lily and Paige and Bailey onto a plane to South America.

It wasn't until I got closer to the water tower that my eyes picked up a light in the distance. It was really faint and small, but it was definitely a light. I headed my bike out that way.

The ringing in my ears had been replaced with the throaty sound of my bike engine. The light got closer and closer, and then suddenly stopped. Whoever it was must have heard my bike and turned off the lights. That's okay. I was close enough to find it anyway.

The full moon was just over the mountains now, and that definitely helped things. I was getting pretty close when I saw the unmistakable sight of taillights. The lights had been from a car, and that car was leaving!

Just then, in the sky, I saw the lights from a small airplane coming down toward us. Good. GOOD. That meant I wasn't too late. I just had to catch the damn car before they had a chance to load the girls and Paige onto the plane.

I cranked it up and went even faster. I didn't dare look down at the speedometer, but it felt like I was going faster than I'd ever gone before. I started to think about what to do once I caught up with them. I probably didn't have the handgun on me anymore, as whoever knocked me out probably took it with my phone. I might still have the switchblade in my boot. It was gonna be old-fashioned hand-to-hand combat. I had no idea how I was gonna do it, but failure was not an option here.

The brake lights on the vehicle came on, which meant they were stopping. There would be no way for them to load people onto an airplane without stopping the car and getting out, so I'd been ready for this.

Just as I'd suspected, the plane flew low over our heads, circled, and then landed in a makeshift air strip in the middle of the desert, and stopped facing the same way it had come. I figured I had about five minutes tops to deal with however many people were in the car and on that plane. My sister and

Bailey weren't likely to be much help, and I didn't know about Paige's fighting skills, but I didn't imagine they were great, so I was gonna have to channel my inner Jackie Chan and take on all of them at once.

I'd taken Tae Kwon Do as a kid, but I'd never really imagined I'd use it in real life.

As soon as I got close enough, I jumped off my bike and ran to the SUV. The plane was idling and there were two guys that came out of the plane speaking Spanish. It was hard to see in the dark, but I think that El Diablo was the only one in the SUV, other than the girls and Paige. One of the girls must be lying down, though, because I could only see the shadows of two of them in the back seat.

The side door to the car opened, and El Diablo grabbed someone from the inside of the car. This was my moment to act.

"El Diablo! Stop!" I yelled, not because I thought he would stop, but to act as a diversion. Since there were three of them and one of me, as far as I could tell (there might be others in the plane or the SUV) I figured it was best to just pick the guy closest to me and circle around him so that the others were directly behind him.

The guy in front was tall and skinny and was wearing some kind of black jacket and a baseball cap. The guy behind him was really big, like a linebacker. He was the kind of guy who was strong, but not fast. El Diablo was facing Baseball Cap, and had Bailey out of the car, trying to hand her off to him.

I got a good running start and slammed into Baseball Cap and then did a roundhouse kick to Diablo's face. Linebacker then came running toward me, and I dodged him, and ran in a circle, in front of Baseball Cap again. When he got to his feet, I grabbed him by the jacket and pulled him to me, swinging him down to the ground in front of Linebacker.

"Ryder!" Lily called to me from the car.

"Stay there!"

Bailey wisely climbed back in the car and shut and locked the doors.

Diablo roared back to his feet at the same time Line-backer lunged for me. I dodged out of the way and ran around to the other side of the car, using it as a shield.

I bent down to feel in my boot for my switchblade and it was there. But if I had a weapon, they probably did too. I needed to stay on my toes.

"Let them go, Diablo," I said, brandishing the switchblade.

"Like hell I will," he said, and he lunged for my knife.

I dodged but twisted my ankle on some uneven ground and fell backwards, right into Linebacker. I heard Baseball Cap running back to the plane, likely to get a gun of some kind. Time was running out.

Linebacker was holding me, pinning my arms to my body, and I took the knife in my fist and swung my arm down and plunged it into Linebacker's thigh as hard as I could. I felt the warm spurt of blood right before he started to scream and instinctively let me go. I jumped to my feet and got in a defensive stance.

From a distance, I could hear sirens. Someone had called the police?

Diablo came for me, but my knife was still in Linebacker's thigh, so I threw my best punch, right at his face. He staggered back, but then came at me again, trying to uppercut me, but I dodged his fist.

I was starting to fatigue and wondered how much longer I could fight. From his wobbling, it looked like Diablo was getting pretty out of breath, too.

Lunging at him, I grabbed him and tried to twist him to get him to fall to the ground. I was able to knock him off balance, but as soon as I did, we all heard the unmistakable sound of a machine gun peppering the air with bullets. Baseball Cap was standing in the doorway of the airplane, firing at us.

Dropping to the ground, I yelled, "Lily, get down!" The sound of gunfire kept going and I army-crawled around to the back side of the SUV and crouched behind one of the tires. The sirens were getting closer and closer.

Finally, Baseball Cap stopped firing and just shut the door to the plane. A minute or so later, the plane started to move and began to take off.

"Esperate!" said Linebacker as he heard his ride back to South America leaving. It was too late; the plane was taking off as the police and ambulance arrived. Diablo took off on foot into the desert.

My heart was pounding and I was out of breath as I stood to knock on the car window. "Lily. It's okay. You and Bailey and Paige can come out."

I saw two heads pop up and look out the window. The door cracked open and Lily said, "Is it over?"

"Yeah, honey. Come on out."

Lily came out of the car and straight into my arms. Bailey came out next and stood there awkwardly until I motioned for her to come into the hug, too.

Over their heads, I looked into the back seat of the car. "Where's Paige?" I asked.

"She's not with us," Bailey said.

"She's what?" I said, shocked.

"She's not here. She helped us escape from the motel, but then these guys found us and one of them, the Diablo guy, brought us here, and the other one, the fat one, took Paige with him. Diablo said he could 'have' her and then he was supposed to dump her in the desert."

Oh my God. Paige was still missing.

"Everybody freeze. Put your hands up where I can see them."

We complied, of course. "Who called the cops?" I asked.

"I did," Lily said. "I used that emergency panic button in the car."

"Good thinking."

The whole time the cops were securing the scene and I was standing there with my hands up, waiting for them to realize I wasn't the bad guy here, I was trying to figure out how I was going to find Paige.

PAIGE

I wasn't exactly sure where I was at the moment, as I was in the back room of what appeared to be a restaurant or bar. There were cardboard boxes and crates of things. But from the look of it, none of it had been used in quite some time.

I closed my eyes, wishing I could rub them, but my hands were tied. Watching Bailey and Lily be dragged kicking and screaming into that SUV was one of the worst moments of my life. I had no idea whether they were on a plane to South America at the moment or not.

As soon as that Diablo guy took off with the girls, the guy who'd been holding me let go. I started to run after the car, and he just stood there laughing. His laugh was raspy and his teeth were yellowed. The guy smelled like he hadn't had a shower in weeks.

"You go ahead, cariño. Get all sweaty chasing after that car. I love a little salt on my food."

He then took a disgusting bandana out of his pants pocket and put it over my eyes. The thing smelled like you would imagine, having been stuffed down his pants like that. I thought I was going to puke.

He put me on his bike, blindfolded, and then got on in front of me, and said, "You better hang on, cariño, or you're gonna fall off."

I wasn't sure, but I think he was calling me honey. The last thing I wanted to do was fall off his bike, so I wrapped my arms around his flabby midsection and held on for dear life. My hair was whipping my face, I was blindfolded, and his body odor was practically choking me. I needed to find a way to get out of there.

Thankfully, we only rode for a couple of minutes before I felt the bike stop. He grabbed me and pulled me off of the bike and dragged me into some building, which was where I was now.

Another way I knew it was a restaurant was because I could hear whats-his-name in the kitchen banging around. He'd tied me to a cast iron sink with some zip ties, and so the chances of me getting away at the moment were pretty slim. My poor wrists were bloodied and raw, and I'd cut the back of my arm climbing out the window. And I really had to pee.

"Excuse me?" I said, calling to my abductor. "Can you come here, please?"

He had been humming and somehow cooking something because I smelled food coming from the kitchen. Either he didn't hear me or was ignoring me so I said it louder. "EXCUSE ME?"

"What do you want?" he yelled from the other room.

"I need to use the bathroom."

He walked into the area where I was and was literally eating a bowl of food. It smelled like beans and rice, and lord only knows how old it was because this place appeared to be abandoned. Where did he even find electricity?

"Do I look stupid?" he said through food-filled cheeks.

I didn't give him my honest answer and said, "I really have to go."

"The last time you were in a bathroom you broke out a window. Pee where you are." He turned to walk back into the other room.

"Please? You can leave the door open to make sure I don't escape. I just really need to go."

A wide grin spread across his greasy lips. "Oh yeah. I like that idea. I'll watch you."

He was so disgusting I shuddered. But it was either that or pee my pants. Besides, it would get me out of being tied up.

He set the bowl down on the counter and got a knife to cut me free. For a second I thought about grabbing it, but realized that he was probably better at knife fighting than I was. My dad took a fencing class at the country club once, but that was the extent of our family's weaponry experience.

It only took a couple of minutes for him to free me, and then when I stood up he leaned in really close and took a deep breath. "You smell really good, chica. We're gonna have some fun."

He reminded me of a big fat cat who played with a mouse he'd caught before he killed it. As soon as I thought that, my chest gripped in fear. I needed to get the hell out of here or I'd end up dead, like a mouse.

He grabbed my arm and I winced because his fat fingers poked right where I'd been cut. He dragged me through the kitchen area and I could see that we were indeed in an abandoned restaurant. He'd managed to find a can of Sterno and used it to make rice and beans.

Honestly, the guy looked like he could stand to miss a meal or two and I wondered why he was so desperate to have food that he'd break out scavenged food and eat like we were camping buddies.

"You go in there. Leave the door open and I'm going to watch you."

As I pulled down my jeans, I felt something in my back pocket that made me smile. It was my phone! I thought I'd left it in the car when I went to explore that sound and found the girls. The battery was probably dead, but maybe not. And if not, I might be able to get a text out.

"You smile, huh? You like to be watched?" He was rubbing his crotch and I could see a hard-on growing. I'd better think of something fast, or I was going to be his dessert.

After I finished peeing, I wanted to distract him before he got any ideas, so I said, "Are you a chef or something?"

"No, why?"

"I just wondered because you managed to make some really amazing smelling food in what appears to be an abandoned restaurant." I wasn't even lying. I was so hungry and the food did smell good.

"No, chica. But I did work in a taqueria in downtown LA before I came to La Playa."

"Have you ever been to LBJs in Redondo Beach?"

"Naw, man. Mi familia didn't go to those rich neighborhoods. Unless it was with a can of spray paint." He laughed that raspy sounding laugh again.

"My name is Paige, by the way. Did you know that?"

"No." He got up and grabbed the bowl of food and handed it to me. "Here. Since you seemed to like it."

I really didn't want to use the same spoon as him, but I wasn't about to say no. I took a bite, and it really was good. "This is good. Thank you...?" I left a space for him to say his name.

"Chanclas."

"Like the sandals?" I asked.

"Yeah. My real name is Carlos but when I initiated with my first MC I was wearing chanclas and the name stuck."

"And now you're with Las Balas?"

His eyes narrowed. "How do you know Las Balas?"

"My sister's friend, the dark haired girl from earlier, she is dating one of your prospects." My mind started to wander to where Lily was, but I couldn't worry about that. As long as I kept this guy talking and kept his disgusting hands off of me, I was okay.

"Which one?"

"Scorpion."

"Ah yeah. Weird kid. I don't think he has what it takes to be a Las Balas, but it's not up to me."

He walked across to where I was standing and put his hand out for the bowl. "You done?"

I took the last bite and wiped the corner of my mouth and nodded. "Yeah, thanks."

He turned to put the bowl on the counter behind him and when he turned back, his eyes looked different. The friendliness of just a few moments before was gone and his eyes were vacant and dark, and he took a small pistol and a switchblade out of his boots and unbuckled his pants.

"Okay. Enough foreplay. Take your fucking clothes off."

RYDER

"I really advise that you come with us, sir. You need to be checked for internal injuries." The paramedic was standing in front of the open back door of the ambulance that contained Lily and Bailey. The guy I'd been calling Linebacker was in a different one, under police protection.

It had only taken a few minutes for the officers to find out what had happened. There was a massive manhunt underway for El Diablo, and the entire desert was lit up from helicopters circling the area.

They had given me a preliminary exam and I was fine. What I needed to do was find Paige. "I'm fine. I need to contact the other girl's family. I'll meet you at the hospital."

I climbed up into the ambulance and kneeled down between Lily and Bailey. "They are going to take you to the hospital in Barstow, which is about an hour away. I'll call your parents, Bailey, and tell them you are okay."

"Actually, can you wait a little? They are going to freak out if they hear that Paige is missing."

I wasn't sure about that. I would want to know right away that Lily was okay. The uncertainty must have shown on my face because she added, "We can call when you get to the hospital, okay?"

I nodded. "Okay."

Just then a youngish looking paramedic stuck his head in and said, "Almost ready." Bailey smoothed down her hair and said, "Do I look okay?"

"Your hair is sticking up, but otherwise, yeah," said Lily.

"Oh! That reminds me! I have something for you." I dug in my jacket pocket and pulled out the hair tie and handed it to Lily.

"What's this?"

"Gerard Way gave that to me to give to you."

"What?" she asked, looking incredulous. "You met him?"

"Yeah. At the convention center. He took it out of his hair and told me to give it to you."

She clasped it in both hands. "Oh my God. He WORE THIS?"

I grinned. "And wanted you to have it." I leaned over and kissed her on the forehead. "I love you, Lil. I'll see you in a few hours."

I walked over to my bike and took a look at the helicopters looking for El Diablo. He was either going to get caught, shot, or go so deeply underground that he wouldn't be a threat to us for a long time. Kidnapping two teenage girls with the intent to sex traffic them was a pretty major crime, and when one of them was the white daughter of a high-profile surgeon...he wasn't going to get away with it, even if he did get caught.

I turned my attention to Paige. Where could she be? I figured my best bet was to go to the last place I saw her and try and figure out what happened from there.

It only took a few minutes to get to the Bun Boy Motel. The Audi was still there. The curtain and broken glass were still by the tree. I could see a broken-out window on the second floor.

Since I saw Chanclas with El Diablo and the girls said that "the fat one" was told he could "have" Paige, it made sense that it was him who took her.

He probably only had his bike, so he wouldn't go far with a kidnap victim in the open like that. My best guess was that they were pretty close by.

I went around the other side of the motel to see if maybe they were in a room. But the bike was gone and I didn't hear or see anything. He wouldn't be so stupid as to keep her here, would he?

Maybe it would be a good idea to head over to the restaurant and see who was still there.

Two minutes later, I was there. The only ones who were still around were Hawk, Swole, Chalupa, and Scorpion.

"Did you find them? Did you get there in time?" Scorpion practically ran up to me as soon as I turned my bike off.

"I did. They were just about to be loaded onto the plane, but I got there in time."

"I wondered when I saw all the copters," Hawk said.

"Were they okay? Where they...hurt?" Swole asked.

"They seemed okay, but they're on the way to the hospital in Barstow to be checked out."

"Where's Diablo?" asked Chalupa.

"That's what the copters are doing. He ran off into the desert."

"He's toast," said Swole.

I then turned to Hawk and asked, "Where's Padre?"

"Trainer took him home. He kinda snapped back into reality after a bit."

Memory issues were so weird, and I imagined we were just seeing the beginning of it with him.

"What about Paige?" Swole asked. "Did she go to the hospital too?"

"No. She's still missing. I think Chanclas has her."

"That fat bastard?" Hawk said. "He's more dangerous than he looks. We need to find her ASAP."

"Yeah."

"Is it okay if I go to the hospital to see Lily? I need to make sure she's okay," Scorpion asked.

"I'll take you," said Swole. "I'll make sure that Paige isn't already at the hospital."

"Good thinking," I said.

"We'll go out and look," said Hawk, nodding to Chalupa.

"Too bad you don't have Find My Friends," Scorpion said. "That app is a lifesaver sometimes."

"Oh my God, I do! We added each other before I left." I pulled out my phone. "Dammit. It's dead."

"Here." Swole handed me her backup charger. "This'll take a few minutes but you'll get enough of a charge."

"Thank you!" I said, plugging the phone in.

"I want it back. Tammy will kill me if I lose it."

"Will do." I fist bumped her and then they all rode off in different directions. Now I just had to wait until my phone charged and then hope that Paige's phone wasn't dead too.

It was the longest five minutes of my life as I sat alone in the Bun Boy Restaurant parking lot waiting for my phone to charge enough to be able to turn it on.

I had too much time to think. I thought of my parents

and what they would have gone through tonight with Lily being missing. I wondered what they would think of her and the job I did raising her.

I could almost hear my mother's voice as she said, "I am so proud of you, mijo." Tears sprang to my eyes.

I wanted what they had. She and my dad had loved each other so much. It was one of those fairytale kinds of things where they were always together—even in death.

I didn't want to spend the rest of my life alone. Didn't want to end up like Sofia. I wanted love, like Swole and Tammy, and even Hawk and his wife.

And as much as it surprised me to realize this, I was starting to think I wanted all of that with Paige. She was beautiful and funny and fierce and passionate. She was everything I could ever want in a woman, even though she was way out of my league.

Just then, the parking lot dirt lit up. My phone was on. I entered my password, opened the app, and there it was. The blue dot that indicated where I was (thank you Verizon for the reception out here). But where was Paige's blue dot? "Please let her phone not be dead..."

My heart sank when I only saw one blue dot. Her phone must be dead. But then, I squinted to see, and it looked like there was a second blue dot flashing right under mine. "That's weird. Why would the dots be..."

Then it hit me. She was here. She'd been right here the whole time!

The only place they could be was inside the abandoned restaurant. I ran over to the window and pressed my face against the glass. I didn't see much because it was pretty dark, but it looked like there might be some sort of light coming from the back.

I took off running around the back of the building. The door was ajar, and I could hear voices. I stopped to catch my breath so my panting wouldn't alert them to my presence. I wanted the element of surprise.

"I said take your fucking clothes off." His voice was coming from the kitchen area.

"Look, you really don't have to do this..." That was Paige's voice.

"I don't have to. I want to. And once we get started, you're gonna want it too."

It sounded like a belt fell to the ground and my stomach clenched. I wanted to kill him immediately but I forced myself to be quiet as I tiptoed to the entrance.

He had her backed up against a counter and his pants were down around his ankles. I saw a pistol and a handgun on the counter behind them.

"Please, no. Don't do this." She was starting to cry and he was pawing at her clothes.

"Get your fucking hands off of her," I shouted. Chanclas practically jumped out of his pants. Paige lunged away and I dove for the gun.

Grabbing it, I aimed the gun at Chanclas, who was standing, facing me, with his dick hanging out. "Don't shoot!"

"Like hell I won't." I shot the motherfucker in both knees and he went down hard.

"Let's get out of here. We can call 911 from the parking lot," I said, grabbing Paige's hand.

We ran out the back door, and as soon as we got outside she threw her arms around me. "Thank you! How did you find me?"

"Find my Friends!"

She started laughing through her tears. "Oh yeah!" And then she asked, "But...the girls? Are they...did you...?"

"Yeah. I got there in time. They are on their way to the hospital in Barstow." I then wrapped my arms around her. "It's over, Paige. You're all safe."

PAIGE

"Really, don't come down." I was on the phone with my parents, who had me on speakerphone. Ryder and I were just leaving the hospital. "They're keeping Bailey and Lily overnight for observation and then Ryder and I will bring them home in the morning. The doctors said they are perfectly fine."

"I'd really rather come down, but I trust your judgment, Paige," my dad said.

"I'm so glad you're both safe, honey," said my mom.

After he'd burst in just in the nick of time, we'd called 911 and then headed out to the Barstow hospital. The girls were already in a joint room, watching Keeping up with the Kardashians and laughing about hospital food. We'd all been interviewed by the cops, who'd said they would want us to fill out a statement next week.

"Hawk, you need to make sure that no one else touches it. Only you. Got that?" Ryder was on the phone with Hawk, arranging to get his bike from Baker, since we'd taken the Audi to Barstow.

The engine roared to life as I pulled the car out of the

hospital parking lot. I'd have rather Ryder drove, but my dad would kill me if I let someone he'd never met drive the car. We were just gonna have to change that and make some introductions tomorrow.

But for now, we were going to stay overnight in Barstow. It was a sleepy town halfway or so between LA and Vegas, and because of that, it really only had the kinds of accommodations used by truckers and travelers. No fancy hotels or anything. Frankly, I didn't care. All I wanted was a hot shower, some food, a bed to sleep on...and Ryder.

I was blown away at how he single-handedly managed to save all three of us. It was like something out of an action hero movie, except it was real. This man, sitting next to me, really had risked his life to save me.

When I was in school, I'd read something about attraction between people in an emergency, and I was definitely feeling the spark. But, if I were being real, what was about to happen had been building for weeks.

As we made our way to the Ayres Suites, I stole glances at Ryder's profile. He was quiet, deep in reflective contemplation. He'd been through a lot tonight, too. I could sympathize with the fear of losing a sister to sex traffickers, but not what it would feel like to have it be your only family and at the hands of someone you'd considered a father figure.

Suddenly, it occurred to me. Maybe Ryder's rescue of me was just part of who he was. Maybe it didn't mean anything about feelings for me—he'd have done the same thing no matter who it was. My heart sank a little as I realized that it was true. He was a man of character and strength. He hadn't done it because he loved me; he'd done it because it was the right thing to do.

"Okay, we're here," I said pointlessly as we pulled the car into a space right in the back of the very full parking lot.

There must be a lot going on in the sleepy town of Barstow tonight.

We got out and went to the front desk, and a very old man slowly made his way over from the small chair he'd been sitting on. He appeared to be eating something chewy, because his mouth was full. "Can I help you folks?"

"Uh, yeah, we need..." I looked at Ryder for some clue but he was looking the other way. "We need two rooms."

That got Ryder's attention and he looked at me with raised eyebrows.

"I'm afraid we only got one room left. There's a national bowling tournament in town and we're almost sold out. It's got a king-sized bed, but there's a pullout couch for ya."

I slid the emergency credit card that Dad always kept in the car to the guy. "Fine. We'll take it."

As the man sucked his teeth and droned on about the amenities of the motel, I could feel my body heat rising. One way or the other, Ryder and I were about to spend the night together. We finally got the paper envelope with our keys and made our way over to the elevators. Ryder still hadn't said a word since we'd left the hospital.

Like an idiot, I felt the need to fill the silence with chatter. Finally, after we'd walked down the long hallway, we stopped at the door. "Looks like this is us," I said.

His eyes were cloudy with some emotion I couldn't discern.

"Ryder," I said at the same time he spoke.

"Paige."

We smiled and he said, "Ladies first."

"I just want to say thank you for everything you did and to let you know that I know it doesn't mean anything about me or that you feel anything for me and that the only reason we are here is because we have to get the girls from the hospital tomorrow and that we tried to get separate rooms but we couldn't and it's okay because I'll take the foldout couch and you can have the bed."

He was grinning. "Are you finished?"

I smiled and nodded.

"Are you sure? We could stand out here and discuss how many towels we'll each use and what to do if the toilet seat doesn't have that paper strip across it."

"Too much?" I asked, blushing.

"Personally..." he said, leaning in for a whisper, "I'd much rather go inside, peel off all of your clothes, and lick every inch of that body of yours."

That did it.

My hand was shaking as I tried repeatedly to get the stupid plastic card to make the little light turn green. Ryder placed his hand over mine and guided the key up and down and I swore there was nothing more erotic on the planet.

Finally, the blessed door opened. I turned around to thank him for helping and his mouth closed down on mine before I could get the words out.

The attraction that had been building combined with the intensity of the past few days to create an explosion of desire. We tumbled into the room and closed the door, not even bothering to look around.

Our mouths never left each other as hands grasped at buttons and buckles, kicking shoes off and stepping out of pants.

When there was nothing left but our shirts, Ryder backed me up against a wall, pulled my T-shirt up, kissed my neck, and reached around to unclasp my bra. As he pulled the clothes over my head, it brushed my raw wrists and the glass cut on my arm and I winced in pain.

"You're hurt," he said, taking my wrists and examining them. "Why didn't you tell them at the hospital?"

I didn't want to talk. "I'm fine." I reached my hand down and wrapped my fingers around his stiff, hard cock.

That was all the reassurance he needed, and he peeled off his shirt.

The sight of him naked took my breath away. I'd imagined what he would look like...I'd dreamed about it...but nothing had prepared me for this moment.

His chest was literally perfect. He had several tattoos that I planned to ask about later. His six-pack had the most beautiful trail that led down to a glorious cock that would soon be deep inside of me. His strong biceps were just the right size. Big, but not in that veiny bodybuilder way.

He saw me checking him out and grinned. "You like what you see?"

I was embarrassed for a second and said, "Yeah. You are... really hot." That was the best thing I could come up with? What a derp.

"Let's take a shower," I said, walking to the bathroom. I was fully aware of his gaze on my ass as I walked in front of him. But it had been a long, dirty day and I wanted to get clean.

The water heated up surprisingly quickly and we stepped inside. It was small, but I preferred it that way.

If Ryder looked good dry, he looked like a god wet. His hair was slicked back as he bent down to kiss me. It was actually tender at first, and he took my face in his hands. "Paige. I..."

I reached up to kiss him again. I closed my eyes and our tongues began exploring. His hands ran down my back and cupped my ass, bringing me closer into him. His hard cock pressed against my belly and I wrapped my arms around his neck.

My pussy was starting to throb. I needed him inside of

me. Any part of him, so I took his hand and guided it between my legs.

I was very glad I'd shaved the other night, because my skin was smooth and naked, and I could feel everything intensely.

His fingers instinctively went to both my clit and inside. Moving in and out, following my breathing, he kissed me, pinched my nipples with one hand, and fucked me with his other hand.

The combination was exactly what I loved, and I felt my orgasm building.

"You are so wet, Paige. I am going to make you come and then I'm going to lick it up."

As soon as he said that, my pussy tightened around his hand and a wave of intense pleasure ripped through my body. I lost all awareness of where I was, and the whole world narrowed down to his hands inside of me, pressing all the right spots.

I clung to him, panting, as the pleasure wave rose and fell. "Oh my God. Oh my God." That was all I could say.

I reached down and grabbed him again, but he said, "No. Not yet." He stepped aside and let me rinse off, and then pulled the shower curtain aside as he turned off the water.

I grabbed a towel, handed him one, and dried off a little bit.

He took my hand and said, gently, "Come here."

We went over to the bed and he laid me down at the end. "I want to finish what I started."

Spreading my legs, he kneeled down in front of me. "You're beautiful, Paige. What a beautiful pussy you have."

He then dipped his head down and began licking me. It was so soft that my body twitched. He took two fingers and began moving them in and out of me, licking and lapping my juice. "Your cum is so sweet. I could eat you all night."

I felt another climax starting and I put my hands on his wet hair. "Ryder..."

He knew what I wanted and stood. That magnificent cock was right at the level of my body, and he lifted my knees, spread me open and slid inside.

At first, he didn't move, just savoring the feeling of being inside. He was big and filled me completely. "You feel so good, Paige. So fucking good." He looked me in the eyes and asked, "Are you ready?"

I nodded.

He started moving, faster and faster. He was pumping his cock into me and I lifted my knees, placing my hands under them. I wanted to take all of him.

I was trying to hold out so that he could come first, but I couldn't. Just as Ryder threw his head back and let out a deep growl, another climax seared through my body. I felt him flood my pussy as I clamped down on him.

Time stood still for a moment and neither of us moved. I opened my eyes and saw him looking, not just into my eyes, but into my soul.

He dropped down onto the bed next to me. We were both sweating and out of breath. As I rolled over, I didn't know where things would go with him or how it would turn out. I only knew one thing for sure. I wanted this man, and I wanted him in my life for a very long time.

The rest was just details.

EPILOGUE: PAIGE

Six Months Later

"Can I hold the baby?"

Lily and Bailey were taking turns holding Emory, the baby that Swole and Tammy had finally adopted.

"Don't get any ideas," Ryder said as he sipped on another cup of coffee. "No babies for you for a very long time." He then looked at Scorpion, who now was going by his birth name, and said, "Got that, Scott?"

"Yes, sir." Scott brought over slices of cake for everyone seated at our table. "I'm more interested in finishing prospecting for Outlaw Souls and getting my degree."

We were having an adoption party for Swole and Tammy at Tiny's. I'd quit working here shortly after we left Barstow and my parents had put up the money for the mobile health clinic. We'd been up and running for a couple of months, and Heals on Wheels was starting to get publicity.

We'd partnered up with local senior living complexes, and even managed to get Padre into one of them. It was one of those places that was like a regular neighborhood, but also had increased levels of care for when you really needed it.

Scott and Lily were dating, but casually, since she had a

year to go before graduating high school. He was attending La Playa Community College and Lily was doing a dual enrollment thing so they could take classes together.

Bailey was also in the middle of a lot of senior year activities, and she and Lily had become inseparable.

Fortunately, it was easy for them to spend time together now that I'd finally moved out of Banner Manor and in with Ryder. I honestly thought my parents would give me shit about it, but my mother had fallen in love with Ryder. She called him her "son outlaw."

Since Padre stepped down as the president of Outlaw Souls, Ryder had taken the club in a new direction. They were going to clean up the streets of La Playa. Main enemy number one? Las Balas. El Diablo hadn't reappeared, but it was just a matter of time until he did.

"Paige, look." Swole nodded her head toward the counter. "That is not something I ever thought I'd see." She was looking at Ryder holding Emory and cooing at him. "He looks really good with a baby, don't you think?" She grinned and winked at me.

Little did she know, he was about to get a lot of practice doing just that. "Hey, can I get some more ice cream? I can't get enough to eat these days..."

Read on for a sneak peek of **OUTLAW SOULS BOOK 2** featuring the Treasurer of the MC, Pin, and a whether or not the sparks between him and Claire can survive her big secret. **Buy now!** FREE with Kindle Unlimited.

SNEAK PEEK! PIN (OUTLAW SOULS BOOK 2) CHAPTER ONE

Pin

"Alright, brothers, that's it for me," Ryder said.

I looked up from my bike to see Ryder standing up and brushing off his dark jeans. He nodded at Moves and me as he headed for the door. We had been working on our bikes at the shop for the last hour or so like we did almost every Friday afternoon.

"Aw, you're really blowing us off for drinks again?" Moves asked.

"Yeah, I'm sick of dragging your drunk ass home every night," Ryder snapped.

I smirked down at the ground. I loved it when Moves and Ryder badgered each other. They never meant any harm. It was all in good fun, just one of the things that made us brothers, bonded by our devotion to our club, the Outlaw Souls.

"Pin, I'll see ya later," Ryder said.

He clapped my shoulder as he headed out, his back ramrod straight. Ryder was the type of guy who thought he had to carry the whole world on his shoulders. It showed sometimes in the way he walked with purpose and a hint of weariness.

Once the roar of his motorcycle had faded into the distance, Moves glanced at me. "You're coming to Blue Dog Saloon, right?"

"Wouldn't miss it," I said.

Moves was the enforcer of our group. He had earned that position through a dedication to street fighting that was, frankly, terrifying. Nearly every day, I thanked my lucky stars that he was on our side.

As enforcer, Moves always liked to be in the thick of things, and he never missed a meet-up among club members. It was Friday, so that meant drinks and music down at the Blue Dog Saloon, our unofficial headquarters.

The bar was located on the dingy side of La Playa, far away from the glistening sandy beaches and the boardwalk. Blue Dog Saloon was scrappy but proud, just like the club itself.

"Sweet," Moves said. "Maybe this time you'll actually get a girl's number."

He grinned at me beneath his messy mop of sandy brown hair.

I rolled my eyes. It wasn't that I couldn't get a woman, it was just that I only liked having one for a few nights. I wasn't into all that soul-changing all-consuming type of love. Moves was, but somehow he could never find it. He was always getting his heart broken or breaking someone else's heart and then breaking some noses as well, just to round everything out.

"You don't mean that," I said. "You'd be screwed without my wingman skills."

As I stood up, Moves jokingly shoved me in the chest. I dodged away with a laugh, but patted my chest to make sure my glasses were in one piece. Moves had already broken my accounting glasses three times in the last six months and I was sick of getting replacements.

I had been the treasurer for Outlaw Souls for over three years. I kept my glasses on me at all times in case I needed to crunch numbers at any point. We always had gigs, odd jobs, and fundraisers, so keeping track of all the influx and outflow was no joke.

I was happy to do it though; the club was everything to me. I had been born and raised on the wrong side of La Playa. Sick of my mom's non-stop fighting with her boyfriend, I had joined up as soon as I was eighteen. I was never the guy to grab the center of attention, so I had always wanted to be treasurer – not in the middle of things, but still pulling strings behind-the-scenes.

I remembered when the older guys had suggested I get an accounting degree at a local college, I'd been almost offended. I thought they were trying to get rid of me or hint that I wasn't suited for a biker club. Instead, they explained that they needed someone with certain skills and, since I had done so well in high school math courses, I had potential.

I had done well in math because it was a good distraction from whatever jerk my mom was seeing that month, but I didn't tell them that. Instead, I got into an accounting program with the club paying for the whole thing. They didn't ask for a single penny back. That's when I knew I would do anything for the Outlaw Souls. It's been almost ten years since I first asked to join, and I feel the same way.

I grabbed my leather jacket with the patch and pulled it on as Moves gathered up his stuff. He looked at his phone and then up at me. "Kimmy just texted, she's headed that way as well."

I rolled my eyes. Kimberly Delasante was a pledge who hated – absolutely hated – being called "Kimmy." So, of course, Moves called her nothing else. Kim was a tough girl though, and always gave as good as she got with Moves.

Moves and I pushed our bikes out into the bright sun of

La Playa. It would start to set soon, so we had just enough time to go for a quick ride and grab dinner before heading to Blue Dog.

The auto shop we liked to work out of was on the corner across from a rundown taco place and a loan's office. The taco place needed a serious paint job and had grimy windows, but we all knew that they were the best tacos outside LA. There was another, shinier version of La Playa, but it wasn't for me, never had been.

"Seriously, man, I worry about you," Moves said as the sun hit us.

It was pretty out of the blue, so I raised my brows.

"You got walls a mile high, brother," Moves continued. "Being single is fun for a while, but come on, you don't wanna be grabbing beers with your brothers every Friday for the rest of your life, right?"

To be honest, I kinda did, but I wasn't going to admit that to Moves. Beneath his battle-hardened exterior, he was a total romantic. He believed in soulmates and all that bullshit.

I wasn't going to be the one to tell him that true love didn't exist.

Because it didn't. I had known that since I was five years old and my dad walked out, leaving my mom weeping on the floor of our shitty little kitchen.

I hadn't seen my dad since. Hadn't wanted to. Even when Ryder and Moves suggested I try tracking him down, for closure, I wasn't having it. Some stones are better left unturned.

Not to mention that while I didn't have many memories of him, I had enough to know he wasn't worth knowing. I remember waking up to his drunken ranting late at night, and I remember him constantly losing a job but blaming someone else for his unemployment. It was never his fault. His boss was always a prick, or his friend threw him under the bus, or my mother was such a nag and drove him crazy.

My mother loved him, she really did. But that never did her any good, just made her hurt all the more when he betrayed her. Unfortunately, my mom fell in love easily. She fell in love with the next guy, and the next, and the next. And she always ended up crying with her broken heart in her hands.

The truth was, people weren't good enough for each other. One way or another, someone always cheated or walked out or lied. So I was happy to flirt and engage in the occasional fuck, but why bother with anything else?

I wanted my life to be like the numbers on my accounting books. Even, balanced. No lies. No evasions. No room for slip-ups.

Moves shrugged at my silence. He was used to it. I had never been much of a talker.

"Still waters run deep," Moves mumbled.

I pushed my sunglasses on as we mounted our bikes.

"What about Kimmy?" Moves blurted out. "She's cute, right?"

I snorted. Moves had never been subtle. Also, I was pretty sure he was the one with a thing for Kim, he just didn't know it yet.

"Definitely not my type," I said. "Besides, she's seeing someone."

"She is?" Moves asked.

"Yeah, I heard her telling Carlos about it the other day," I said. "Older guy, I think. Big corporate job, sounds like."

"Fuck," Moves said. "I guess someone is willing to risk getting close to that bitch on wheels."

I rolled my eyes at Moves' ever-changing opinions. The guy had more mood swings than a teenage girl. "You just said she was cute."

"Yeah, well," Moves said. "I say a lotta things."

I pushed my dark hair back from my face and rammed my boot down on the pedal. I was getting sick of chit-chat, even if Moves mostly meant well.

Moves started revving his own engine and our bikes roared to life.

As we hit the open road, I couldn't hold back my grin. We merged onto the highway and headed south. If we were to go straight west, we would hit the ocean. That was one of my favorite rides, but we didn't have time.

I leaned forward and urged my bike even faster. The feeling of the wind pulsing over my face as my bike picked up speed was what I had fallen in love with first. The club and the brotherhood had just been added bonuses.

I figured between my bike and my brothers, who needed anything else?

SNEAK PEEK! PIN (OUTLAW SOULS BOOK 2) CHAPTER TWO

Claire

I tossed the envelope onto Veronica's desk with a dramatic sigh. "Men are idiots."

"Tell me about it," Veronica said, not even looking up as I flopped into my desk chair.

"This guy was legit emailing his mistress naked pics from his personal phone that is part of his family plan, which his wife is on," I said. "She gave me all the passwords so logging on was a breeze. She could have done it herself."

"Claire, baby, they *never* want to do it themselves," Veronica said. "It's easier if we swoop in and find the dirty stuff for them."

I shrugged and kicked my feet up on the desk. When I had first landed the job at Daniel O'Malley's private investigating firm, I had been excited. Following cheating husbands with big sunglasses and a fancy camera had been thrilling.

But after three years, it was getting old. I could practically recite the result of every case brought to us by some weeping wife.

Her bigwig husband had a mistress, who was probably

under twenty-five and had massive tits. He thought he was so clever by using a burner phone and telling his wife he had to work late. We usually only had to trail the husband for a few days before we could get back to the wife with photos, emails, texts, and other pieces of evidence that her divorce attorney would know how to use.

Occasionally, there was something a little more riveting. Sometimes a missing child, a guy who owed money and was trying to disappear, or even a murder that the police couldn't crack. But for the most part, it was asshole husbands.

Veronica swung her thick dark hair over one shoulder and gave me a wry smile. "Think Dan got another one in today. It'll go to you though. I'm not done working on this one."

I raised my eyebrows. Veronica usually sped through her cases. While I preferred to trail the guys and gather evidence off of phones or hard drives, Veronica did it the old-fashioned way. She'd put on an itty-bitty black dress and waltz right up to the scumbag at the bar. A few hours later, she would be in his hotel room, plenty of photos taken for the poor wife, and lecturing the guy on being an idiot.

"You're kidding," I said. "This guy said no to you?"

"He's a careful one," Veronica said. "Doesn't drink either, which is always a challenge."

"You'll get him," I said.

"I always do," Veronica said with a wicked gleam in her eye.

Veronica and I were the only two employees who worked for Dan. She had been at the firm for almost a decade and had pretty much taught me everything I knew.

I had been green when I arrived in La Playa with twenty bucks in my wallet and a thirst for adventure. I had wanted to try being a stunt double in Hollywood or a personal assistant for a millionaire. Anything that would offer adventure really.

I grew up in a small town in Northern California. My parents were nice, but ordinary. By the time I graduated from the local college, I was desperate for something new and exciting. So I headed south and never looked back.

Working as a PI was exciting. It was. I loved the life I had created for myself in La Playa. But lately, I had been chomping at the bit for something else. A bigger case. A new challenge.

"You ok?" Veronica asked.

She was observant, that's part of what made her a great PI. She had noticed my sense of ennui.

"Sure," I said with a small shrug. "Just bored."

"If you're always looking for the next thrill," Veronica said. "You'll miss all the good things you've got."

"Thanks, Yoda."

Beneath her femme fatale exterior, Veronica was wise and sympathetic. She was the uncontested best at breaking the tough news to the wives of the cheaters. I was always too abrupt. I would just shove the photos in their face, telling them the man they had been married to for years sucked and they needed to move on fast.

Veronica was more understanding. She held a lot of hands, wiped away a lot of tears, and gave amazing pep talks about how this wasn't the end, it was a new beginning. I knew that if I ever got gutted by a cheating husband, I would run to Veronica first.

Not like that would ever happen though. After the bull-shit I had seen in the last few years, long-term relationships looked about as appealing as a dumpster fire to me. Besides, every guy I dated ended up boring me. I always got tired of the same old routines.

The door swung open and Daniel O'Malley strutted into the office. He was over six feet tall, his suits were always wrinkled, and his hair was always messy, but he had managed to build a successful private investigating business over the course of two decades. He said it was because he had always hired smart and capable girls like me and Veronica.

I swung my feet off my desk and straightened my oversized jean jacket.

"Fenelli," he barked at Veronica. "Still working the Greenberg guy?"

"Yup," Veronica said.

"Brennan?" he asked, turning to me.

Daniel always used our last names. I think it made him feel like he was in an old-school Hollywood detective movie.

"Finished with the latest today," I said. "Just need to type up the report."

"Great," Daniel said, tossing a file onto my desk. "I've got a new one."

I opened it up. Olivia Cook was concerned by her husband Trey's recent behavior. She wanted to get to the bottom of it, as painful as the truth may be. I scanned the pictures. Olivia looked like something out of Town & Country magazine. Blonde hair, big smile, floral dress, cute kid clinging to her hand.

Trey also looked the part. Handsome face and a build that suggested he had been an athlete in high school but was just starting to go to seed a bit. Guys like that gained a few pounds, got a few gray hairs, and their fragile masculinity exploded. They had to go out and shower some dumb young bimbo with gifts to get their self-esteem back on track.

"Wonderful," I said. "Another thrilling chapter in the book of matrimonial bliss."

Veronica stifled a giggle, but Daniel frowned.

"Let's 86 the sarcasm, Brennan," Daniel said.

I flashed him my most charming smile. "Sure thing, boss. I'll get right on this tonight."

Daniel gave a brisk nod and headed into his office. He gave off a stern exterior, but he was a good guy overall.

I settled into my desk and pulled out my notebook. My desk was a mess of papers, photos, and pens, but I thrived in that kind of disarray. Veronica, on the other hand, kept her desk immaculate.

Two hours later, I had finished putting together my final report. I sent it to Daniel and then grabbed the next file. As tired as I was with the cheating husbands, I always got a little thrill of anticipation with a new case. It was like a wrapped present where you *thought* you knew what it was, but you couldn't be sure.

Anything could lurk beneath the shining veneer of Trey and Olivia Cook. It could be scandal, intrigue, a web of deceit that stretched back years. He could be the head of a coke ring or the leader of some crazy cult. No matter what it was. I, Claire Brennan, would crack the case.

It was probably just a mistress with big tits. But it could be something else, and that's what gave me the little flutter of butterflies in my stomach.

I read over the info about Trey's office and license plate number. I checked my watch. If I hustled, I might be able to trail him as he left his work. It was Friday night, so if he was meeting his side chick, it would be about now while his wife was at home making mac and cheese for the kid.

I shoved the file into my bag and stood up.

"Heading out already?" Veronica asked.

"Might as well," I said. "Who knows? This one could be different."

Veronica smirked. "Maybe."

Fifteen minutes later, I was parked outside his office in the heart of La Playa near the boardwalk. He had a nice cushy position in a consulting firm; probably had a corner office too.

I rolled down my window and kept my eye on his car. When I first started the whole PI thing, my instinct was to do it like the movies. Big sunglasses, a hat, maybe even a scarf. But the secret to not being seen is to not try and hide. Just dawdle about in plain sight. Look like you're up to absolutely nothing.

It doesn't hurt that no one suspects foul play from the petite girl with a blonde ponytail.

Veronica does it a little differently. She wants to be seen. She wants the guy to notice her so much that he can't resist. Not me. I stick to my corners where I can watch undetected.

At six on the dot, Trey Cook strolled out of his office and hopped into his car. In the distance, the sun was setting over the water. He was working late for a Friday, but maybe he did that to cover his bases if his wife ever asked a coworker.

If I were a betting woman, I would have put my money on Trey heading straight to one of the bougie cocktail bars or steakhouses in downtown La Playa. Mistresses loved that kind of thing while men like Trey loved to impress.

It's a good thing I didn't gamble, because Trey surprised me by driving all the way out to East La Playa.

"Ok, Trey," I muttered. "We're roughing it tonight."

He finally pulled up to a bar I had never been to called *Blue Dog Saloon*. It didn't look dangerous, per se, but it was decidedly shabby. Not without charm, though.

I cast a wary eye towards the bikes parked outside. There were biker clubs all around LA, but I had never had any trouble with them. Then again, I had never really gone near bikers.

Overall, it was not the type of bar I expected Trey to frequent. This case was looking more interesting by the second.

I looked down at myself. I was wearing worn black jeans with frayed hems, sturdy boots, and my reliable jean jacket.

Not exactly a Friday Night Out Look, but any PI worth her salt is always prepared for wardrobe adjustments.

I pulled my hair out of its ponytail and ran my hands through it until it settled in soft waves down to my shoulders. Then I dug around in my bag and yanked out some dark red lipstick and mascara.

After hastily applying the makeup, I shoved my wallet and my phone into my smaller handbag. It looked weird to walk into a bar with a huge tote bag. Getting pictures would be tricky, even if I used my phone instead of my nicer camera.

I shoved my small pink pepper spray into my purse as well. I was pretty street-smart and I knew how to avoid risky situations, but a girl could never be too careful.

At the last minute, I tugged my jean jacket off. I was wearing a white lacy blouse with short sleeves, cropped to show just an inch of my stomach. If I needed to flirt my way around the bar that would help.

Veronica had taught me how to keep everything I might need for any venue in my car. She also always had at least three pairs of heels, but I skipped that step. I never wore heels. They made it too hard to run if things got dicey.

I pulled myself out of the car and walked towards the entrance. There was a cute hanging sign of a blue dog with rock music blasting from within. I burned with curiosity. What was Trey up to?

Once inside, it didn't take me long to figure it out. I casually scanned the room as I headed towards the bar and spotted him right away. In his button-down shirt and tie, he stood out like a sore thumb.

He was holding hands with a drop-dead gorgeous woman. She had legs for days and raven-black hair. I blinked in surprise when I saw she wasn't in the typical Mistress Fashion. She was wearing a black leather jacket and jeans, introducing Trey to a few guys who wore matching leather jackets.

I felt a pang of sympathy. I bet she didn't even know the jerk had a wife. Most of the mistresses were aware of a wife, they just don't care or they think he'll leave her someday. Sometimes they honestly don't know, and those were always tough.

This girl looked way too self-respecting to be with a married guy. It was unlikely she knew.

I leaned on a chair and waited for the people in front of me to finish ordering. I furrowed my brow as I tried to come up with a plan of action. Snapping photos was risky in a bar since people would notice.

Plus, Olivia would want more than a few blurry pictures. It's amazing how wives, even the smart ones, can justify damning photo evidence. They needed it to be undeniable before they believed their beloved husbands have betrayed them. I would need to trail Trey a bit more, and maybe dig up some texts.

I could also try and approach the girl on her own. It was risky, and it sometimes backfired to enlist the mistress, but it could pay off. Especially if she had a taste for revenge. I glanced back at the tall beauty and observed her flashing eyes. Definitely looked like the revenge type.

"Hey, can I get you a drink?"

I stifled an eye roll as I turned around at the masculine voice. Then blinked in surprise when I saw a leather jacket beneath a cocky grin. The same leather jacket Trey's side piece was wearing. What a delightful surprise. I could see the patch on the arm now. Outlaw Souls.

I gave him a sweet smile and shrugged. "I'll take a Corona."

Within minutes, the biker had gotten both of us a beer. He had to know the bartender.

"I'm Claire," I said.

"Pleasure," he said. "I'm Moves."

He jerked his head and led me back towards his friends. I took a deep breath. It was beyond risky interacting with the person you were trailing too early in the game. Veronica never put on her itty-bitty dress until she had gathered all the information she needed.

Luckily, Trey had let the woman lead him out onto the dance floor while Moves was steering me towards a few of the guys perched at a table in the corner.

"Claire, this is Hawk and Carlos," Moves said. "And this is Pin."

I glanced at the guys as they nodded at me. They all had nicknames. I had heard biker clubs used alternate names, but I had always doubted it since it seemed a little cheesy.

Hawk and Carlos seemed nice and relaxed, but the third guy, Pin, looked like he had just swallowed a wasp. He clasped his lips together and barely gave me a nod. My eyes lingered on his broad shoulders and glowing tan skin before I turned back to Moves.

"So, you new in town?" Moves asked.

"No, I've been here a few years," I said. "I work in sales downtown."

My father used to say that I lied like a rug. Only he had told me it was a weakness. I had learned it was my greatest strength.

"What brings you out here?" Moves said.

"Meeting a friend," I said. "I'm just a bit early."

In fifteen minutes, I could glance at my phone and either say my friend had bailed or, if I needed an escape route, say she wanted to meet somewhere else and head for the exit.

I looked up at Moves just in time to see him widening his eyes at Pin and nodding at me. So Moves was the wingman for a very reluctant Pin. Interesting. I could work with that.

I pulled myself up into the chair next to Pin (where I still had a good angle on Trey and his girlfriend) and gave him a smile.

"So, *Pin*," I said. "How'd you get that name?"

CLICK HERE To Read FREE with Kindle Unlimited!

LEAVE A REVIEW

Like this book?
Tap here to leave a review now!

Join Hope's newsletter to stay updated with new releases, get access to exclusive bonus content and much more!

Join Hope's newsletter here.

Tap here to see all of Hope's books.

Join all the fun in Hope Stone's Readers Group on Facebook.

ALSO BY HOPE STONE

All of my books are currently available to read FREE in Kindle Unlimited. Click the series link or any of the titles to check them out!

Guardians Of Mayhem MC Series

Book 1 - Finn

Book 2 - Havoc

Book 3 - Axle

Book 4 - Rush

Book 5 - Red

Book 6 - Shadow

Book 7 - Shaggy

ABOUT THE AUTHOR

Hope Stone is an Amazon #1 bestselling author and Kindle Select Allstar award recipient who loves writing steamy action packed, emotion-filled stories with twists and turns that keep readers guessing. Hope's books revolve around possessive alpha men who love protecting their sexy and sassy heroines. When she's not writing binge-worthy books she's a full time "work-at-home" wife and mother of 3 kids, 2 crazy dogs (Nika and Fritz) and 2 badass black cats (Jade and Thundercat).

Learn more about all my books here.

Sign up to receive my newsletter. You'll get free books (starting with my two-book MC romance starter library), exclusive bonus content and news of my releases and sales.

If you liked this book, I'd be so grateful if you took a few minutes to leave a review now! Authors (including myself) really appreciate this, and it helps draw more readers to books they might like. Thanks!

RYDER: AN MC ROMANCE
Book One in the Outlaw Souls MC series
By Hope Stone

Made in the USA
Middletown, DE
14 October 2021